Andrew Glass

Tales and traditions of Ayrshire and Galloway

Andrew Glass

Tales and traditions of Ayrshire and Galloway

ISBN/EAN: 9783337174323

Printed in Europe, USA, Canada, Australia, Japan

Cover: Foto ©Andreas Hilbeck / pixelio.de

More available books at **www.hansebooks.com**

TALES AND TRADITIONS

OF

AYRSHIRE AND GALLOWAY.

BY

A N D R E W   G L A S S,

AUTHOR OF "POEMS AND SONGS," ETC.

G L A S G O W:

DUNN & WRIGHT, 47 WEST NILE STREET.

1873.

TO

JAMES SCOTT HENDERSON, Esq.,

LONDON,

This Volume

IS RESPECTFULLY DEDICATED, AS A GRATEFUL TRIBUTE FOR MANY

ACTS OF KINDNESS RENDERED TO

THE AUTHOR.

PREFATORY NOTE.

THE reader of these tales is not to suppose that, because they bear the title of "Traditions of Ayrshire and Galloway," they possess little interest for the public, apart from that district of Scotland. Intelligent readers are aware that every tale must have a locality, and that if the imagination is allowed too wide a range, the author, no matter how great his literary attainments, fails to produce the effect intended. If the subject which the writer selects is skilfully managed, it will find a sympathetic response in the hearts of men at the antipodes. Burns' Mouse and Daisy are common-place subjects, yet they excel, in my humble opinion, the greatest lyrics of any of our living poets, who generally delight more in high-sounding phrases than the language of the heart.

Let not the reader suppose. that I wish to impress him with the idea that there is something strikingly original in this little book. By no means. I know its shortcomings as well as paterfamilias is supposed to know the faults and failings of his children. I may briefly say, however, by way of enlisting the reader's sympathy, that the tales were written under all the disadvantages incidental to a wandering life, whilst representing the press in the west and south of Scotland. But if the public accord to this book the kind reception which they gave to my "Poems and Songs," I will be not only grateful, but endeavour shortly to bring before them tales of greater length, and deeper interest.

ANDREW GLASS.

GLASGOW, *8th May, 1873.*

CONTENTS.

TALES AND TRADITIONS.

THE LAIRDS OF LUGAR.

AN AYRSHIRE TALE.

CHAPTER I.

AYRSHIRE is so rich in legendary lore that the great difficulty of a writer is to make a suitable selection from the rich field of antiquity. Every stream has still standing, on its banks, the ruins of feudal fortresses, and the classic Lugar is no exception to the rule. Long anterior to the development of the mineral wealth of the county, when Cronberry was the haunt of the peesweep and plover, and the Lugar sang its moorland song to some lonely bondsman tending his chieftain's herds, there stood two castles on its banks, in sullen grandeur, which time and the ruthless hand of man have destroyed.

The Castle of Auchinleck, long since in ruins, stood on a projecting rock of red sand-stone, formed by the junction of the Hill-end burn with the classic Lugar. A portion of it still remains, and is surrounded on the Lugar and opposite side by deep precipices. The other two sides are accessible by steep ascents, the old zig-zag approaches upon which are still traceable. The bridle-road, as it was called, from the Castle of Ochiltree, wound in a similar fashion over the hill which intervenes. On the opposite side of the stream, but a very little higher, stood the Castle of Ochiltree—equally strong and impregnable. Not a vestige of it, however, now remains. But of this more anon.

Towards the close of a mild April evening, Elspie Grant sat alone, in an isolated cottage, on the outskirts of the village

B

of Cumnock, gazing listlessly at the dying embers of a peat
fire. On the hob, at her side, sat an over-grown tom-cat,
purring and dressing his whiskers, while on a small oaken
table at her elbow, lay a silken scarf emblazoned with the
twelve signs of the zodiac. The chair on which she sat was
formed of black oak, and embellished with most strange
devices, such as the crescent moon surrounded with a halo of
stars; a death's head and cross-bones, with the inseparable
appendage of an hour-glass. Elspie could trace her genealogy
to the Druidical priesthood, and had the dangerous reputation
of being an adept in all the occult sciences, as well as versed
in the art of sorcery. By the villagers she was avoided as
much as possible, and by the clergy she was hated on account
of her superior education, and her religious mode of life—
having never been known to attend mass or confession. This
open defiance of ecclesiastical authority would have been a
dangerous experiment for Elspie in those days had she not
been under the especial protection of the powerful Patrick
Dunbar—the patron of the church. How this friendship commenced and continued between the Laird of Blackcraig and
this singular lady none cared to inquire. Once Jamie Gow—
who was ostler at the London, and an especial favourite,
ventured to pop the question concerning Sir Patrick's intimacy
with her, but he was often heard to aver, when half seas
over—when sober he never referred to it—that he would
never do so again.

As the shades of evening deepened around her, Elspie
arose from her listless, dreamy attitude before the fire, went to
the door and looked out, then returned inside and lighted a
small lamp, and again sat down with her face towards the
door, as if anxiously expecting a visitor. In the course of a
few minutes some one approached the door and rapped
timidly at it.

'Come in!' cried Elspie, in a commanding tone of voice.

In obedience to the summons the door opened, and a young
lady entered with a hesitating step, and glanced anxiously
around her. She might be eighteen years of age, and wore
her hair in waving tresses, according to the fashion of the
period. The features were regular, and there was a faint
glow on the cheek, and an intelligence in her dark eyes which
rendered her positively handsome.

'What would'st thou with me, Phemie Colvil?' asked Elspie, as she rapidly scanned her fair visitor.

'Ha! you know my name,' cried the maiden, with a start, which did not escape the quick eye of Elspie.

'Of what use would be my knowledge if it did not enable me to discover such a trifle as this; but pray be seated, and state your business to me frankly and fearlessly. If I can aid thee in any enterprise I will be most happy to do so.'

Thus encouraged, Phemie cast her eyes modestly on the floor, and said she was in love, and that she was most anxious to learn if she was beloved in return.

Elspie arose from her seat, and, approaching the young maiden, fixed on her a keen searching look as if she was in the act of dissecting every lineament and feature. Blushing and borne down by this close examination on the part of one whose expression was so commanding, Phemie bent her eyes on the ground, and did not again raise them till in the act of obeying the command of the sorceress—'Look up, and be not afraid, but hold forth thy hand.' Elspie inspected her palm, according to the form of the mystic arts which she practised, and then heaved a sigh and said, 'Thou wilt not be successful in this love affair.'

No patient ever watched the countenance of his medical attendant, when death or life hung on his word, with greater anxiety than Phemie did the face of Elspie during the brief time she inspected her hand; but when she pronounced the words which blighted the hopes of her heart, she fell to the earth with a wild despairing cry.

'Holy Mother! I might have expected this when she ventured into my accursed den,' muttered Elspie, as she bent anxiously over her, and applied the usual restoratives.

In a few moments Phemie opened her eyes, and looking fixedly at Elspie, who was endeavouring to raise her up, she murmured in a despairing tone, 'Let me lie where I am, I cannot live without his love.'

'But you shall live!' exclaimed Elspie firmly, as she assisted her to rise, and again seized her hand, 'See, here the line of life is deeply marked and clear, which indicates a long and prosperous career.'

'How can a life be prosperous which is blasted at its commencement?' asked the maiden bitterly.

'Listen to me,' replied Elspie. 'The ways of Heaven are inscrutable. Could you be happy with a man who loves another? True, you have been led to suppose, from early associations, that the young Laird of Auchinleck regarded you with the same partiality and love as you entertained for him——'

'Then you also know to whom I have given my heart?' cried Phemie, interrupting her in evident astonishment.

'I do.'

'Tell me this then, thou strange woman; does he love another?' asked Phemie, as she looked imploringly at her.

'Nay, as for that I could not say—he never consulted me,' answered Elspie, evasively. A faint gleam of hope irradiated, for a moment, the pale face of Phemie at this answer, and mentally she resolved never to despair of winning the prize upon which she had set her heart.

Elspie seemed to divine what was passing through her mind, for she said encouragingly, 'You are right to persevere, for fate and chance are words, persistive wisdom is the fate of man.'

'Thanks for these words of comfort. Believe me, I shall both remember and act upon them. In the meantime accept of this trifle for the trouble and annoyance I have caused you;' as Phemie said this she threw her purse on the table, and prepared to depart.

'I will have none of thy gold, girl,' said Elspie haughtily, as she lifted the purse off the table and reached it to her.

'This is unkind,' remonstrated Phemie, 'but I must bid you good night; my father is at the Loudon Arms, and I must accompany him home.'

Elspie bade her good night, closed the door after her, and muttered as she returned to her seat before the fire, 'Lucy Dunbar will be more than a match for thee.'

CHAPTER II.

FACING the old churchyard, which occupied the space now known as the Square of Cumnock, stood the Loudon Arms. Sandy M'Phun, the landlord, if the *Auchinleck Manuscript* is to be relied on, was a super-excellent innkeeper. His urbanity of manner and rubicund smiling face had won for him golden opinions from both rich and poor. In his manner there was nothing mean or sycophantic, and he would have formed an admirable contrast to many publicans, who are all things to all men for the sake of inducing them to tarry long at the wine. It would be certainly wrong to affirm Sandy was indifferent about public patronage, but he had an opinion of his own, which he was ready to maintain against all customers. He had another indispensable ingredient in the composition of a good innkeeper: he not only set your wine before you with a cheerful face, but he helped you to drink it with great gusto.

Towards the evening of the day on which our tale commences, Sandy M'Phun stood at the door of his celebrated hostelry, arrayed in plush breeches, blue tunic, and white vest —the latter garment was rather short, and he was continually twitching it down over his capacious stomach. His rubicund face always wore a mirthful expression, but as he observed the. Lairds o' Lugar—as he was pleased to term Auchinleck and Ochiltree—advancing towards him, there was a merrier twinkle in the eye, and a broader smile on the face.

' Glad to see ye, gentlemen, baith looking sae weel. I was juist thinking, as I saw ye coming alang thegither, that ye were rare types o' Jonathan and David,' said M'Phun, as he led the way into his comfortable parlour.

' We're bound thegither wi' a rape as it is, and wha kens but the bond may become stronger yet,' observed the Laird of Auchinleck, alluding to their castles being so contiguous to each other, that a rope suspended across the stream communicated with both houses, and with the aid of a pulley, presents were often passed between them.

' Wha kens, indeed,' said the Laird of Ochiltree, with a broad grin, for the muscles of his face seldom relaxed into a pleasant smile.

' But I'm afraid,' continued Auchinleck, ' Ochiltree will bo driving ower hard a bargain for his bonny dochter.'

' A guid article always commands a guid price,' observed the landlord, laughingly.

' That observation's worth a bottle o' wine, at the least,' cried Ochiltree, rubbing his hands delightedly.

' I suppose, laird, ye'll hae nae objections to buy ane when that's the case,' said the landlord, winking across the table at Auchinleck, for he knew him to be as fond of money as his neighbour was careless and prodigal of it.

'He'll hae nae scruples, at anyrate, about the drinking o't, if I buy it,' said Auchinleck, laughing, and treading on the landlord's foot below the table.

'Oh! as for the matter o' a bottle o' wine amang frien's, it's neither here nor there, sae, landlord, bring in a drap o' the best.'

'With much pleasure, gentlemen, for I'm as dry as an Arabian sandbank,' said Sandy, as he hastened to execute the order.

As soon as the door closed, the Laird of Ochiltree said, in a whisper, 'I dinna want to discuss oor affairs before M'Phun; he's a nice enough body, but he wad laugh at Mess John, supposing it wad ruin his trade.'

'I like him a' the better for his independence; but if the subject is not to be discussed before a frien', in Gude's name, let it drap for ever.'

'I didna mean that at a',' said Ochiltree, deprecatingly.

'And what did you mean?'

'Simply this, that if ye didna close wi' my terms, the least said sunest mended.'

'And what is your terms, my dear auld friend?' asked Auchinleck, sneeringly, for the word *terms* grated harshly on his ear.

'Ye wad hae nae objections, I suppose, to gie me ten hunner merks, if I was giving the han' o' Phemie to yer son.'

'Ten hunner merks to you, an' twa three thousand to them to start hoosekeeping wi', I'd see ye——'

'Fou first,' said the landlord, completing the sentence, as he placed the wine on the table.

'I'm glad ye came in, Sandy, for Ochiltree and I were getting that warm, in this cosy room, that we require something to cool us.'

'I ask yer pardon, gentlemen, for detaining you frae what's profitable to me, and agreeable to you, but I had to attend to Lucy Dunbar. Ye talk about Phemie, Ochiltree, but I wish ye saw Lucy to-night. Ye wad see a vision that couldna be surpassed in Mahomet's paradise.'

'What can hae broucht her doon frae Blackcraig at this time o' nicht?' asked the Laird of Ochiltree, thoughtfully.

'It's no late. Daylicht's scarcely awa', an' she's well mounted,' observed the landlord.

'That's no' answering my question, Sandy,' persisted Ochiltree.

'I canna answer yer question, laird, for I never speered her business, but yer frien', Auchinleck, micht be able to gratify your curiosity; she's often a visitor at his hoose.'

" She'll be likely doon wi' some message or present frae her faither, to that auld witch, Elspie Grant,' said Auchinleck, in a careless tone.

'Ye that kens a' the outs and inns o' Cumnock, landlord, can ye tell me oucht aboot this Elspie Grant?' inquired Ochiltree.

'No,' answered the landlord, as he assumed a serious look for a moment, which sat with a bad grace on his merry countenance.

At this moment the door of the room was opened by Jamie Gow, who informed the Laird of Ochiltree that his daughter, Phemie, was waiting for him at the bar.

'I maun bid ye guid nicht, then, frien's—I suppose, Auchinleck, ye'll no' accompany me up for a wee yet.'

This was spoken in a manner which said as plainly as possible—'I don't want your company.'

'I'm ower comfortable where I am, to think of jogging yet,' said Auchinleck, as Ochiltree departed, in company with his winsome daughter.

For a considerable distance they rode side by side without exchanging a syllable, each buried in their own reflections. Indeed, her father's taciturnity was a source of great pleasure to Phemie, for, after listening to the prediction of Elspie, she felt disinclined to speak at all. If not destined to be the wife of the young, handsome Laird of Auchinleck, the earth contained nothing, in her estimation, worth living for. From her girlhood up, she had been taught to regard Auchinleck in the light of a lover, but the sybil's emphatic utterance had dissipated the happy dream, and rendered her most miserable.

'Phemie,' said her father, abruptly addressing her, 'I was speaking to Auchinleck aboot his son and you to-night, but I didna hear his sentiments richt oot, before we were interrupted by that claverin' body M'Phun.'

'Did he not receive your proposal favourably?' inquired Phemie, in a low voice.

'He thinks my terms rather hard, dear Phemie; but before his son commenced to ride and hunt sae muckle wi' Lucy Dunbar, he wad hae jumped at my offer like a cock at a grosset.

I understan' there's to be a great gathering o' sportsmen at Blackcraig to-morrow. If ye like, I'll escort ye thither, an' we can see an' judge for oorsels. Let me hearken in your lug, Phemie, before we reach the hoose, if I find Auchinleck and his gallant son playing you an' me fause, I'll gie them a deevil o' a surprise some o' these dark nichts—but here we are at hame—recollect no' a word o' this to yer mither, or she'll be ower tellin' Leddy Auchinleck, as she ca's her, a' aboot it, when we're a' awa' at the hunt.'

Phemie promised to obey his instructions, so they separated for the night.

CHAPTER III.

THE seat of the noble family of Dunbar, who were supposed to have sprung from the Saxon kings of England, was Blackcraig. It occupied the summit of the knowe on which the village of New Cumnock stands. The stones of the stately edifice were long ago removed for building purposes, and those walls which are said to have frequently sheltered the saviour of Scotland— the noble Wallace—have now been replaced by a Free Church.

At an early hour on the morning following the incidents contained in the last chapter, all was bustle and excitement at Blackcraig. Gradually the court of the castle began to fill with knights and ladies, attended by their squires and pages arrayed in gorgeous liveries, from the surrounding district. Conspicuous among the gentry assembled, on this memorable morning, was Willie Crawford of Lochnoreis—now Dumfries House. Rumour whispered that Crawford regarded Phemie Colvil of Ochiltree with marked attention, but Phemie either would or could not observe this, owing to her passion for young Auchinleck.

After partaking of a hearty breakfast, amidst the merry sound of the huntsmen's horns, and the baying of hounds, the gay cavalcade sallied forth from the castle, and took their way along the Afton. Whether by chance or pre-arrangement, Lucy Dunbar found the young Laird of Auchinleck riding by her side, while, by another strange freak of fortune, Phemie was accompanied by Willie Crawford.

The morning was beautiful, and every brake and bush was vocal with music, while a thousand wild flowers shed their fragrance on the air. The surpassing loveliness of the landscape and the mirth of the company were calculated to dispel the gloom of the greatest misanthropist; yet, fair as the scene was, it failed to infuse joy into the heart of Phemie Colvil. A hundred times she wished Willie Crawford at the antipodes. Right before her rode Auchinleck and the fair Lucy Dunbar, and every time her rival's silvery laugh reached her ear, it sent a chill to her heart; and although in courtesy she seemed to listen to the Laird of Lochnoreis, yet in reality she heard him not. Lucy Dunbar was, on her part, as merry as the birds which warbled in the brake, and as lovely as the flowers that shed their fragrance on her path. Beside her rode the man on whom she had bestowed her affections, and her heart partook of the joy and gladness which surrounded her.

'Methinks the scenery along the Afton would contrast favourably with any in Scotland,' observed Lucy, as they advanced up the vale, and its magnificent grandeur began to develop itself.

'I have had little opportunity of contrasting it with other localities; but, of this I am satisfied, there is one flower on its banks this morning which would be called the Queen of Afton, had I the right to bestow the title,' said Auchinleck, looking admiringly at his companion.

'Flatterer!' exclaimed Lucy, smiling. 'What would Phemie Colvil say if she heard you make such a confession?'

'Phemie seems to have made a captive of the Laird of Lochnoreis, yet, poor girl, she is looking anything but happy this morning,' said Auchinleck, looking back at her.

'Nevertheless he is not her choice,' said Lucy.

'How do you know that, Queen of Afton?'

'I was down seeing Elspie Grant last night, and Phemie was there also.'

'Getting your fortunes spaed, I suppose—they say she's clever—I think I must pay her a visit, and learn if I'm to have the great happiness of wearing the fairest flower on the Afton in my bosom,' said Auchinleck, looking admiringly on Lucy's face, which was suffused with blushes.

At this moment the shouts of the huntsmen proclaimed that a fox had broken cover, and was careering across the waste moorland, in the direction of Lugar. Conversation was now abandoned for the excitement of the chase, and as Lucy was splendidly mounted, and an expert and fearless rider, she was

soon in advance of the whole party, closely followed by Auchinleck. Over deep ravines; along steep hillsides; through dense
thickets of wood; past swamps and morasses swept Reynard,
closely followed by the hunters. Still Lucy led the chase until
they nearly reached the Lugar.

'See that cursed minx hoo she skims ower the heath, wi'
her hair streaming behint her, like a witch riding on a broom-
stick, through the air,' observed the Laird of Ochiltree, who
had now rejoined his daughter; 'deil than she may break her
neck.'

Scarcely had the wicked wish escaped his lips, when Lucy's
horse stumbled and fell, and she was thrown with fearful violence to the earth.

In a moment Auchinleck was by her side. Springing from
his horse he bent anxiously over her, but to every appearance
she was dead. He called her by the most endearing names, as
he raised her in his arms and pillowed her head on his breast.
Her pallid lips were stained with blood, and had it not been for
a slight pulsation of the heart, he would have thought the vital
spark had fled. In the meantime all who had witnessed the
accident had ridden up to the spot, and amongst others, Ochiltree and his daughter. Phemie no sooner beheld Auchinleck
bending over Lucy in mute despair than she whispered—
'Father, this is nae place for me, I canna endure this torture.'

'True, Phemie,' answered the laird, 'we dinna seem to be
wanted here. Let us be jogging.'

Sir Patrick Dunbar raised his eyes, for a moment, and
looked at the laird and his daughter as they rode from the spot
where the beloved Lucy was lying, apparently dead; but in
that look was concentrated all the hatred and contempt the
human countenance can express.

'Jamie,' said the elder Auchinleck to his son, 'lift Lucy
gently and bear her across the Lugar to the Castle, it's a wee
bit farther awa' than the Laird o' Ochiltree's, but I'm sure she'll
receive every attention and skill we can command.'

'Thanks, laird, believe me this act of kindness will never be
forgotten,' said Dunbar, in a husky voice.

'Hoots, Sir Patrick! it's only what I wad dae for the
puirest outcast that ever trod the hills o' Scotland.'

'I know it, Auchinleck,' said Sir Patrick, as he grasped his
hand warmly.

In the meantime the younger Auchinleck had crossed the Lugar, and was ascending the steep ascent to the castle, bearing Lucy in his arms, as safely and as easily as if she had been a child, closely followed by the rest of the hunting party.

Sir Patrick waited until he saw her safely laid on a couch, in the Castle of Auchinleck, then bending over the unconscious Lucy, he kissed her gently. For a moment she opened her dark eyes and looked wistfully in his face, and then closed them as if weary of the world.

'Order me a fresh horse, Auchinleck,' said Sir Patrick, while tears glistened in his eyes; 'I must have Elspie Grant here to see my child. If skill and medicine can save Lucy's life, she will snatch her from the grave.'

The assembled group cast on each other strange looks, but none dared to dispute his opinion, although all thought that the skill and advice of a priest would have suited better. No sooner, however, was a horse led round to the hall door than Sir Patrick mounted and rode off rapidly in the direction of Cumnock, which, as he neither spared whip nor spur, he soon reached. Elspie was standing at her cottage door as he rode furiously up, and seeing his distracted look, and his horse covered with foam, she exclaimed—'You are the bearer of evil tidings.'

'I am. Come inside and shut the door.'

CHAPTER IV.

HOWEVER strange and inexplicable it may be, we all have, at times, presentiments of approaching danger. Some unseen messenger seems to whisper, Beware ; and a vague undefinable fear takes possession of the mind, which we in vain endeavour to shake off. When the crash comes we are ready to exclaim —'We knew some calamity was about to overtake us.' True, these apprehensions serve no earthly purpose which we are aware of ; but as sickness and old age are said to prepare us for death, so these gloomy forebodings may, in a certain degree, prepare the mind for the misfortune when it comes. Be this as it may, Elspie Grant, from the moment she had parted with Lucy Dunbar, on the previous evening, had felt an unaccountable dread of coming evil; and when Sir Patrick rode up to her door, as described in the last chapter, her worst fears were realized.

'In the name of heaven what has occurred, Patrick?' exclaimed Elspie, as she shut the door and stood trembling before him.

'Be seated, Elspie, and compose yourself, for you'll require all your courage and self-possession.'

'Speak out, man, plainly, and tell me at once what fresh misfortune is in store for me. This suspense is worse than death. What of my dear child?'

'She was living when I left Auchinleck, ——'

'But she may be dead now,' she cried, interrupting him, 'is not this what you would say?'

Sir Patrick bowed his head on his hands and remained silent.

'Our sins have found us out,' she exclaimed, bitterly. 'But why sit moping there? Up, man, instantly, and bring me a horse from the Loudon Arms; by the time you return I will be ready to accompany you.'

While Sir Patrick hastened to obey Elspie's commands, she quickly divested herself of the coarse garments she usually wore, and arrayed herself in a superb riding habit of dark silk velvet; then quickly opening a chest, she took from it a few vials containing medicines of various kinds, which she carefully secured about her person; put on a hat which suited her dress, locked the door, and waited impatiently Sir Patrick's return. So complete was the change in her appearance, that not one of the gossips of the village recognized in the haughty looking lady the despised and avoided Elspie Grant.

Sir Patrick immediately returned, and, without speaking a word, he assisted her to mount; when, to the great astonishment of the idlers about the doors, they rode off at a furious pace in the direction of Auchinleck Castle.

'If Lucy Dunbar's mother was living I wad swear that lady was her,' observed the landlord of the Loudon Arms, who was standing at his door when they passed.

'They're as like each ither as twa peas,' answered Gow, the ostler, sagely.

'Did Sir Patrick no' tell ye wha she was, when ye were getting the beast ready?' asked the landlord.

' No. Nor I didna ask him, for he seemed in nae humour to answer questions,' answered the ostler.

' I had the same opinion o' him mysel', Jamie. Noo, awa' an' gie Meg a rub up, for I think I'll take a turn up the water and see Auchinleck. I hae been thinking a' morning about him and the Laird o' Ochiltree.'

It would have been much better for both lairds if Sandy had been employing his mind upon any other subject, as will shortly appear.

While Elspie Grant and Sir Patrick Dunbar were pursuing their way to Auchinleck Castle, with Sandy M'Phun, the jolly landlord of the London Arms, following in their wake, let us take a hurried peep into a room in the Castle of Ochiltree. Beside the laird sat his idolized daughter, Phemie. Evidently she had been weeping, for her eyes were inflamed and swollen, when a servant entered and announced the Laird of Lochnoreis.

' Dry your e'e, Phemie, for I think he'll be the bearer o' joyfu' news to us baith,' said the laird in a low voice to his daughter; then turning to the retainer, he said—' Show the laird in.' Crawford had scarcely entered the room, when Ochiltree said—

' I'm truly grateful to ye, Lochnoreis, that ye were sae considerate as come across. Is Lucy living or deid?'

' She was living when I left; but if I hae any skill, her tenure o' life is unco short.'

' Thank God!' mentally ejaculated Ochiltree; but he added aloud, ' I'm truly sorry for the sweet creature. It's a sudden call. I hae been reasoning wi' Phemie here on the impropriety o' taking it sae sair to heart, for she has dune naething but sit and greet since she cam' in.'

' This is extremely foolish, and serves nae purpose,' said Lochnoreis, looking affectionately at the sad face of Phemie.

' Is she conscious, or has she spoken a word since she fell?' queried Ochiltree.

' Conscious!' reiterated Lochnoreis; ' when I left the hoose it would be impossible to tell whether she was leevin' or deid.'

' Hech sirs! is she sae near the gates o' death as that. It maun certainly be a great trial for Sir Patrick.'

' Sir Patrick's not there, but he's expected every minute alang wi' Elspie Grant.'

'Ha!' exclaimed Phemie, breaking silence for the first time, 'I wad gie a hundred merks to hear her opinion when she arrives.'

'An' I wad gie anither, Phemie,' cried the laird, excitedly.

'Ye're on guid terms wi' Auchinleck, I suppose, laird,' observed Lochnoreis; 'sae ye'll better step across the Lugar and see and hear for yersel'.'

'I wadna dae that for a thousand merks—an' folk say I'm fond o' siller—and I'll tell ye my reason. When I saw her lying insensible, and young Auchinleck sae tenderly bending ower her, I was for asking them to carry her here, it being nearer, and on this side o' the water; but it instantly flashed on my mind—Sir Patrick's a great man, and if I ask them to bear his bairn here, Auchinleck will be offended; and, believe me, laird, I wadna quarrel wi' sic an auld tried freen for ony baby-faced leddy on the water. But dae ye no' perceive if I was gaun ower an' speerin' about her noo, some ill-natured body micht misconstrue my motives, which I wadna hae dune for the world.'

'Thank ye, laird! thank ye!' cried Lochnoreis, enthusiastically, grasping his hand. 'This manly, straightforward avowal raises ye higher in my estimation than ever ye stood before. I looked at yer action frae a different point o' view a'thegither; an', to tell ye the truth, I wasna half pleased at ye, for I thocht yer conduct unneighbourly.'

'Ay, Lochnoreis, but there's aye twa ways o' looking at onything. Bless me! when I was your age, my imagination aye galloped twice as fast as my reason, and I was eternally arriving at wrang conclusions; but time and experience teaches fules. I daresay gif ye had been in my place to-day ye wad hae asked them to the house, and made an auld freen a bitter enemy. But I kent better, my lad—I kent better. Phemie, lass, awa' an' bring ben a drap o' my best wine.'

Phemie hastened to obey his orders, and as soon as she was out of hearing, Ochiltree approached the young Laird of Lochmoreis, and told him, quite in a confidential whisper, that he didna like to ask him before Phemie to return to Auchinleck and bring them the news, but after he had partaken of a refreshment he would take it as a great favour if he did so, and by the time he returned dinner would be ready. So adroitly had Ochiltree managed this *aside*, that the young laird, after drinking a glass or two of wine, returned to Auchinleck to learn Elspie Grant's opinion of the extent of the injuries Lucy had sustained. As soon as he saw him safely across the Lugar, Ochiltree returned to the house, mentally resolving that if Lucy did not die from the effects of the fall, he would find another method of shortening her days.

CHAPTER V.

HOLDING up the skirt of her riding habit with her left hand, Elspie Grant walked into the apartment where Lucy was lying, pale as marble and motionless as death. Casting a rapid glance around the room on the ladies and gentlemen assembled, she approached the couch where Lucy was laid, and bending over her, put her hand gently among the tresses of her dark auburn hair. When she withdrew it her fingers were stained with blood.

'Just as I thought, Sir Patrick, from your description of her state,' said Elspie, looking up. 'She has fallen on her head, and concussion of the brain is the consequence.'

'Is there no hope, then?' asked Sir Patrick in despairing accents.

'Life and death are in the hands of God,' replied Elspie, reverently. 'Two things, however, are necessary to her recovery—she must not be removed from this house, and I must get a bedroom for her where no sound will disturb her rest.'

'Both are at your service, lady,' said Auchinleck.

'Thanks! Now all may retire, but her father and our kind host. I wish to administer a little medicine.'

Willingly would the younger Auchinleck have remained, but he had no alternative but lead his friends into another apartment. As soon as they had retired, Elspie ordered Lucy's father to raise her head a little, then taking a vial from her pocket she poured a few drops into a teaspoon, containing water, and administered the restorative. Instantly a slight tinge of colour returned to Lucy's face, she opened her eyes languidly, and a faint smile of recognition illumined her countenance.

'Thank God there's hope!' exclaimed Elspie. Tears of gratitude streamed down Sir Patrick's face, while his lips moved in prayer, heartfelt and sincere, to the beneficent Ruler of the universe.

'Now,' said Elspie, addressing Auchinleck, in a low voice, ' let me see the bedroom you can give us, for I intend to be the nurse myself.'

' The room which I am going to show ye,' said Auchinleck, as he led the way into an adjoining apartment, 'is unknown to every one in the castle wi' the exception of my wife and son, but it's baith quiet and comfortable.'

'That's all that is required, I care nothing for its mystery,' said Elspie. Auchinleck went to the farthest corner of the apartment in which they were standing, and looking attentively at the oak wainscoting, he pressed his finger against what appeared like a dark knot in the wood, and immediately a door flew open, disclosing an apartment, well lighted and furnished, which overlooked the deep ravine at the base of the castle.

' You have only to press this spring here and the door can- not be opened from the outside. The contrivance is simple, and was constructed for safety. Now come with me and I'll let you see another way of egress from the room.' As Auchin- leck said this he led them to the opposite side of the apartment, and opened a door which disclosed a flight of stairs leading to the bottom of the glen.

'A most ingenious contrivance,' exclaimed Sir Patrick.

'Assist me, gentlemen, to remove Lucy. This room is every- thing I could desire,' observed Elspie.

Her request was at once obeyed, and as she signified her desire to be left alone with her patient, Auchinleck and Sir Patrick withdrew.

In the hall they found the greater part of the hunting party, with the addition of Sandy M'Phun of the Loudon Arms. Lochnoreis waited no longer than he heard there were hopes of Lucy's recovery; but hastened across the Lugar to impart the joyful news to the Laird of Ochiltree and his winsome daughter.

' I'm truly glad to hear it, for she's a sweet bit lassie,' said Ochiltree, trying to smile, but the effect was a complete failure, and to the great astonishment of Lochnoreis, Phemie commenced to weep.

' Leave the room instantly, Phemie, and get the dinner served up. She's a tender-hearted thing, Lochnoreis,' said

Ochiltree, as soon as Phemie retired. 'Joy or real affection on sensitive natures has much the same effect as grief. She'll be a crown o' glory to some puir man—but whist! here she comes like a queen wi' her maids behint her.'

Although Ochiltree pressed his guest to eat and drink heartily, yet he scarcely tasted the food himself. Phemie sat silent during the repast; and although the laird made desperate efforts to be communicative and jocular, Lochnoreis felt happy when the meal was over, and he found himself on the road home. He still retained his penchant for Phemie, but he thought she had some cause of sorrow apart from Lucy Dunbar's illness.

If there was lamentation and mourning, mixed with jealousy and revenge, in the Castle of Ochiltree, in the Hall of Auchinleck mirth reigned supreme. Sandy M'Phun told some of his best stories, whilst he quaffed the laird's rarest wines; and his suggestion that Auchinleck should send over, in a neat parcel, a clean picked sheep's head, as a marriage present from her intended father-in-law, was received with rapturous applause. The heartless cruel manner in which he had acted in the morning towards Sir Patrick Dunbar and his beloved daughter embittered every one present against him, and although Auchinleck said little, he mentally resolved his son should never wed his daughter.

It has become a proverb ' when drink's in wit's oot,' therefore the suggestion was no sooner made than the laird acted on it. Ordering his butler to scrape a sheep's head as bare as possible of flesh, he had it made up in a neat parcel, put into the basket attached to the rope, which was suspended across the water, and which joined both castles. On this strange present was simply written ' The first instalment of Phemie's tocher.' Amidst hilarious bursts of laughter the parcel was dispatched.

Little did the senders dream of the terrible consequences of that joke.

It was now evening, and the Laird of Ochiltree stood on the battlements of his castle, not admiring the peace and beauty of the scene around him, but planning how he could make Auchinleck and Ochiltree one estate. This could only be effected by the marriage of his only daughter with the heir of Auchinleck, and if Lucy Dunbar recovered, which he fervently prayed she would not, he saw little prospect of his dearest dream ever being accomplished. Whilst his mind was distracted and torn with the evil spirits—avarice and jealousy—he observed the well-known basket crossing the water. In a moment he descended from his lonely perch, and rushing into the hall he summoned Phemie to come out and see the present from Auchinleck. By the time they descended the steps leading to the water, the basket had reached its destination, so, bending down, Ochiltree lifted the parcel out and read the fatal words, *'The first instalment of Phemie's tocher.'*

'It's a' richt yet, Phemie dear. Ye thoucht I was drivin' ower hard a bargain, but I should ken better than ye aboot things o' this kind. Lichtly won lichtly worn. Eh, Phemie? Let's awa' into the hoose and see hoo muckle siller he has sent ower. Likely, yer bonny rival's deid.'

Phemie's face was wreathed with smiles, for the first time during that weary day, as she followed her father inside.

'It's carefully put up, as siller should aye be. Phemie, try if ye can unloose it, for I declare I'm quite nervous.' As the laird said this he handed his daughter the parcel.

'If there's siller in this, there's no muckle o't, for it feels unco licht,' observed Phemie, weighing it on her hand.

'Loose the string, lassie, loose the string, an' then gabble till ye're weary,' cried her father, impatiently.

The cord was unloosed, the paper carefully opened, and then, oh! horror of horrors, a bare sheep's head lay grinning at them.

With an imprecation, which we dare not repeat, Ochiltree rushed from the room, whilst Phemie, perceiving at a glance the utter annihilation of all her hopes of happiness, gave a long loud piercing scream and fell insensible on the floor.

CHAPTER VI.

APRIL had given place to May, and by many 'Phemie's tocher' was forgotten. Under the fostering care of Elspie Grant, Lucy had so far recovered that, in a few days, her father purposed removing her to Blackcraig. As there was no pretext for remaining longer at Auchinleck, Lucy had to acquiesce; although she would willingly have remained at it for ever— containing as it did the idol of her virgin heart. Both her father and Elspie divined the reason of her unwillingness to leave, but as they both approved of her passion for the accomplished young laird, and as she seemed to be perfectly happy in his company, they were averse to disturb such a pure source of pleasure to them both. As soon as she was enabled to leave her bed, he was constantly by her side, and in the seclusion of the apartment, overlooking the picturesque banks of the Lugar, they wove many a happy dream. Whether ever they were destined to be realized or not remains to be seen. While Elspie was busy compounding and preparing her medicines, in the adjoining apartment, words of love were spoken and kisses stolen, far more efficacious in restoring Lucy to health than any elixir ever distilled.

' Who can he be, Jamie, that I see every evening strolling around the castle, muffled up in a cloak? See, yonder he is now walking on the opposite side of the glen and looking in this direction,' said Lucy, to the young laird, pointing at the same time in the direction of the stranger.

' I couldn't for the life of me guess, dear Lucy, but likely he's some poor invalid from Cumnock or Auchinleck.'

' I doubt it. There's something in the man's inquisitive look that fills me with alarm,' said Lucy, shivering.

' Lucy dear, if he's a source of uneasiness to you I'll go now and order him off the grounds.'

' I wish you would; for I have observed him repeatedly of late, always wandering about in the gloaming and scanning the castle.'

' You should have told me of this before; but you need not be alarmed about a solitary stranger, he cannot harm you in this eyry.'

' It's not myself I'm thinking about, but you. How do you know but a vindictive bad man, like Laird Ochiltree, might meditate revenge.'

' Sick fancies, dear Lucy, but I'll see who he is.'

Elspie now entered the apartment and told her fair charge she would have to retire for the night, as the evening was getting chilly. Auchinleck bade them good night, and then sallied forth in quest of the mysterious stranger, whose wanderings around the castle were so offensive to Lucy; but although he looked for him, until night shut out the landscape from his view, he never crossed his path. Concluding that he was right in his conjecture, and that the stranger had left for Cumnock, he retired for the night, and was lulled to sleep by the song of the stream beyond his window.

Deep silence reigned throughout the castle, but as the night advanced the wind arose and moaned with a weird-like voice around its turrets. How long Elspie had slept she had no means of knowing, when she was awoke by Lucy shaking her, and asking if she did not hear a strange noise in the lower part of the castle.

Suddenly there came a lull in the storm and they distinctly heard the fierce imprecations of men and the loud clashing of swords.

'Merciful Heaven!' exclaimed Lucy, springing out of bed. 'The castle is attacked.'

'Lucy, listen to me and be calm,' said Elspie, approaching her, and taking her gently by the hand. 'Remember, our only chance of safety depends, not on our strength, but on our courage. The first cry you give will guide the ruffians to our retreat. Be brave—be firm—and thank God your father is at Blackcraig, along with the Earl of Douglas, else he would have shared the fate of all who are known to be in the castle——'

Elspie was interrupted by a crash of swords, accompanied by the yells of men engaged in a life and death struggle in the corridor leading to the adjoining apartment; this completed Lucy's terror, and she fell fainting into her nurse's arms. It was well for her she did so, for it sealed her senses to one of the most fearful crimes of that terrible night.

Auchinleck seeing his followers cut down, as they rushed half naked from their beds, by Ochiltree's fierce retainers, endeavoured to reach the secret apartment containing Elspie and Lucy, but he was so hard pressed that he found it impossible to do so. Determined to sell his life as dearly as possible, he turned to bay in the corridor, and several of his assailants fell beneath his sword, but alone, faint and wounded, he was forced into the room adjoining Elspie's.

'Ha! brave Auchinleck,' cried Ochiltree, triumphantly, 'I'll reward ye noo for the marriage portion ye sae kindly sent my dochter!'

'Cowardly assassin!' exclaimed Auchinleck, defiantly. 'Cause your bandit cut throats to stand aside, an' I'll soon square accounts wi' you.'

' On him, my brave men ; cut him doon whaur he stands.
Weel dune, M'Turk, gie him anither like that in the ribs ; ha !
he's doon. Stand aside, lads, an I'll hae the honour of dealing
the death blow.'

But the honour rested with M'Turk, for before the
cowardly ruffian sheathed his dagger in his heart, the spirit of
Auchinleck had fled for ever from the scenes of earth.

' Thanks, lads ! ye hae revenged yer maister's wrangs nobly,
but my vengeance is only half satisfied. Sir Patrick Dunbar's
bonny dochter is in the castle, unless she has managed to mak'
her escape since the fecht commenced. Noo the man wha
brings the Queen o' the Afton to me, deid or alive, wull be
rewarded wi' a hunner merks and my lasting friendship into the
bargain,' cried Ochiltree.

Elspie listened, pale and horror struck, until the last footstep
ceased to reverberate in the corridor, and then she turned her
attention to Lucy.

' My dear child,' she murmured, bending over her, ' the worst
of this fearful night is over, unless they set fire to the castle, but
even should that be resorted to we have the means of effecting
our escape by retreating down the stair leading to the glen.'

' And be captured at the bottom,' sobbed Lucy.

' I didn't mean to go to the bottom, dear; could we not sit
on the stair supposing the castle was burning ? '

' I care not, Elspie, where I sit or where I die. Likely we
are the only survivors belonging to the castle. Oh, what is to
become of me if Jamie is among the slain.'

' He may have effected his escape,' said Elspie, endeavouring to instil a confidence into Lucy she did not feel herself.

' He may, but oh ! my hopes are faint of such a happy
possibility,' cried Lucy, wringing her hands.

' Then, if he has not, if all have perished, and the castle
continues to be occupied by these fiends, your father will fall
into the trap,' cried Elspie, wringing her hands despairingly.

Never had Lucy beheld Elspie lose command of herself to
this moment, although she had known her from her infancy ;
but, seeing despair pictured in her face, she threw her arms
lovingly around her neck, and said, ' If such is the will of God,
I will have no friend on earth but my dear brother.'

' And your poor, unfortunate mother, now sobbing on your
bosom,' said Elspie, in a paroxysm of grief.

CHAPTER VII.

LUCY regarded Elspie with astonishment. Was it really possible, she thought, that this strong-minded woman had been driven mad by the wild carnage of the night? She looked quite sane, yet her words proclaimed her to be mad. She had heard that this malady assumed many phases: that some who were beggars imagined themselves to be kings. ' Poor Elspie!' she murmured, in her most winning, soothing tones, ' you cannot be my mother in one sense; in another, you have been more than one to me. But this fearful night has disordered your mind.'

' My dear daughter, whom I brought forth in secrecy and shame, listen to me. The crisis of my destiny has arrived, and to-night I must unfold the tale of my life, for to-morrow it may be too late.'

Lucy regarded her compassionately, for she was now convinced that her kind friend and benefactress was really labouring under some strange delusion, induced by the murder and rapine which reigned around her; but to humour her she took a seat by the smouldering fire, and told her to proceed.

' When James I. led his armed bands against the Lord of the Isles, I was a child. My unfortunate father's family were all cut off in the ruthless war which was waged against Macdonald of the Isles, but through the humanity and intercession of a holy man who accompanied the king's army, I was spared and sent to a convent to be educated. Under the abbess, Helen Leslie, I made rapid progress in all the branches of education taught; and, being of a studious cast of mind, I read every book relating to art and science which the nunnery contained. When I arrived at the years of maturity, I was asked to renounce the world and take the veil, and, knowing of no source of pleasure outside the walls of the holy establishment, they easily prevailed on me to give my consent. But scarcely had I become a nun, when an incident occurred which was destined to change the whole current of my life, and which made me deeply regret the vows I had taken. Our convent was situated upon a rocky promontory overlooking the sea, and one of our greatest sources of enjoyment was gazing at the goodly ships sweeping round the bold headlands on which it stood. Towards the close of a fearful stormy day in September, the abbess called our attention to a pleasure yacht, which evidently was in momentary danger of being dashed to pieces against the rocks. Inexperienced as we were, it was evident to us all that she was unable to round the rocky headlands. It was a perfect hurricane, and repeatedly she seemed to be engulphed in the waves, and when she rose again on the crest of a billow she was nearer to the treacherous shore. Seeing she was doomed to destruction, we were permitted to descend the precipitous rocks, to lend any assistance in our power to any one who might reach the shore. Before, however, we had scrambled down, the vessel had struck, and all but one had either been dashed to death against the rocks, or had sunk to rise no more. I was standing on a projecting crag, with the sea fuming in its fury at my feet, when I perceived a young man borne on the crest of a huge wave, past the spot where I was perched, into a narrow creek. Quicker than I can express myself in words, I saw him borne back with the rebound of the wave, and stooping down, regardless of consequences, I grasped him by his raven locks as he swept past, and dragged him out of the sea. He was quite insensible, and fearfully cut and bruised; but he was carefully carried to the convent, and as I had rescued him from the waves, I was appointed to wait upon him. For some weeks his life was despaired of, but, thanks to his youth and a robust constitution, he soon recovered. I will not dwell on what followed. I had never seen a really handsome man before, and long ere he avowed his love for me, I had given him my heart; and on the night he bade adieu to our island home, I fled from the convent and accompanied him to Edinburgh. That man was Sir Patrick Dunbar, and the woman who so deeply sinned you see before you.'

' Oh, merciful heaven, then I am your daughter!' exclaimed Lucy, weeping bitterly.

' You are, but you were born in wedlock, although it was a secret marriage. I retain the proofs of it.'

' Then why does my father not recognize you as his wife?"

' He dare not. The power of the church is omnipotent. I had broken my conventual vows and was anathematized. The lady whom you supposed to be your mother, and whom he married with my full consent, died, as you are aware, in giving

birth to your brother, John, and since I have resided beside
him, assuming the character of an ancient prophetess, or whatever I thought would deter the vulgar from prying into my
affairs.'

'My dear mother, what a hard lot has been thine,' exclaimed Lucy, sobbing on her breast.

'Hard indeed, dear Lucy; but if your father is permitted
to reach us in safety he will be the bearer of a dispensation
from the Archbishop, which will enable me to take my proper
position in society.'

During the time Lucy had been listening to Elspie's strange
narrative, the mirth in the hall became fast and furious.
Ochiltree, under the potent influence of Auchinleck's wine,
insisted that they should finish their fiendish revel in the room
where Auchinleck was murdered; and as the proposal was
hailed with uproarious delight, he led the way along the
corridor.

Elspie and Lucy heard them returning with horror and
dismay; but encouraging each other to be firm and brave, they
crouched down beside the secret entrance to their chamber, and
prepared to listen.

'There lies my hated rival,' cried Ochiltree, as he entered;
'he wasna a bad sodger, but M'Turk was ower mony for him.
Drink this toast, friends, standing—May the nettles sune be
growin' on ilka hearthstane o' oor enemies.'

'Yer ain house is on fire!' shouted a retainer, rushing into
the apartment.

'Ye're a drivelling, idiotic liar. Wha wad dare to fire my
castle? or wha's leevin' that has an interest in siccan wark?'

'Whaur's young Auchinleck?' inquired the retainer, who
was so tipsy that he had to steady himself with the aid of
the door.

'Alang wi' his sainted faither, I hope,' replied Ochiltree.

'He's naething o' the kind,' persisted the serf. 'M'Nab,
wha admitted ye into the castle for the siller ye gied him, tauld
me within this half-oor that he saw young Auchinleck descending frae his bed-room window into the stable-yard, cutting
down twa o' yer best men, takin' a horse frae the stable, and
makin' his escape. It's no my business, laird, but if ye like to
look aboot, ye'll see the glare o' yer castle reflected on
the sky.'

Ochiltree did look about, and beheld an illumination on a great scale. Every shrub and tree was as plainly discernible as if the sun was shining, while the myriads of burning embers, ascending from the blazing castle, seemed like a shower of luminous hail. For a moment he could scarcely believe the evidence of his senses, but, as his mind began to grasp the terrible reality, he drew his sword, and rushing from the room cried on his men to follow him, but the revel had been so long and deep, few of them heeded his command.

'Merciful God,' exclaimed Elspie, 'Thou hast heard my prayer. Lucy, dearest, there is hope.'

But Lucy's heart was too full to express her gratitude in words.

CHAPTER VIII.

CONCLUSION.

BEFORE the younger Auchinleck fled from the castle, he perceived, at a glance, it was in the hands of the Laird of Ochiltree. 'Now for revenge,' he muttered, as he dropped from a window into the stable-yard. Striking the two serfs to the earth who barred his passage to the stable, he seized on his favourite hunter, and started at a furious gallop for the seat of Sir Patrick Dunbar. When he reached Blackcraig the castle was silent and the lights out, but he thundered at the gate until he gained admittance. Being shown to the chamber of Sir Patrick, he briefly related Ochiltree's attack and capture of the castle, and that all had fallen beneath their swords.

'Heaven is dealing hard with me for the sins of my youth, but this is no time to fold the hands, and like a monk, sing peace and rest; stay here until I acquaint the Earl of Douglas, who is my guest, with what has occurred.'

In a few minutes he returned, in company with the noble Douglas, who insisted upon sharing the perils of the night.

Douglas and Dunbar to the rescue! now rang out in clear bold tones throughout the castle, and as the former nobleman never travelled without goodly escort, the chiefs were soon marching at the head of five hundred men.

On the way thither, the young Laird of Auchinleck

expressed a hope that Sir Patrick's daughter and her nurse had escaped, as the entrance to their chamber was unknown to their retainers, and that in all probability Ochiltree would be celebrating his victory in his father's hall.

'I know a method of drawing the fox from his lair,' observed Douglas, grimly. 'Our young friend here would be for marching into the den; but when he has crossed swords with enemies as often as I have, he will depend more on stratagem than valour—although baith's best—I mean courage and cunning.'

'What is your plan, Douglas? for, like Auchinleck, I would be for attacking them where they are,' said Sir Patrick.

'That's quite natural, seeing you have a daughter there, but being no ways biassed by the ties of kindred, I can look at the situation with the eye of a general. But as I perceive you are both impatient, we will proceed to Ochiltree first, make his wife and daughter prisoners—for Heaven forbid we should follow his example—set fire to the assassin's den, and that will light him across the water.'

This was considered to be a capital idea, so ordering the footmen to march at their leisure, they rode rapidly forward with a hundred horse; and upon arriving at the castle, Douglas' plan was instantly carried into practice without any opposition.

In the meantime, Ochiltree, seeing his castle in flames, encouraged his followers to come on, never dreaming of the reception which awaited him on the margin of the Lugar. As they came over the water pell mell, stupid with drink, they fell easily into the hands of the party stationed to receive them. Ochiltree, perceiving his retainers cut down as they reached the bank, endeavoured to fly, but Auchinleck, seeing his intention, dragged him to the feet of Sir Patrick Dunbar and the Earl of Douglas.

'What is to be the fate of this hoary miscreant?' asked Auchinleck, shaking with passion.

'Stain not your sword with the murderer's blood,' cried Douglas. Then ordering one of his troopers to his side, he said, 'Armstrong, I want this knave to dance in the light of his own fire.'

Armstrong needed no further instructions, for putting his hand into his pocket he drew forth a strong cord, threw it expertly over the branch of a tree, run a noose on the end of the rope, and then invited Ochiltree to advance.

'Spare my life, if but for an hour,' pleaded the wretch, falling on the earth and endeavouring to grasp the Earl of Douglas round the legs, but he spurned him with his foot, and told Archie Armstrong to proceed.

'Wad ye prefer to be hung wi' yer face towards yer ain hoose, or juist as ye stan?' Speak the word noo, for the next minute ye'll no' hae a breath to spare,' said Armstrong, as he adjusted the rope about his neck.

Leaving the lifeless body of Ochiltree swinging over the Lugar, the Laird of Auchinleck led the party across the stream into the castle of his ancestors. But we will not attempt to describe the feelings of the young laird as he gazed on the familiar forms lying lifeless, which he encountered at every step on his way to the secret chamber, closely followed by Sir Patrick and Douglas. But, upon entering the apartment where his beloved father was murdered, he was rooted to the spot with horror. Sir Patrick Dunbar, however, broke the spell by advancing to where the gallant old laird lay, and taking his cloak off, he threw it over the corpse, observing as he did so—'They must have been demons and not men who have been here to-night—I tremble for the fate of my beloved wife and child.'

Auchinleck, thus recalled to himself, pressed the secret spring, which had been the means of saving the lives of Elspie and Lucy, and entering, they found them huddled together in a corner of the room.

We will not attempt to describe the scene which followed, but leave it to the imagination of the reader. Some events in one's experience, are indescribable, and the meeting of husband, wife, daughter, and lover, after such a night of horrors, is one of them. After the first joyful emotions of their hearts had subsided, Auchinleck went in quest of the body of his mother, and to his unspeakable joy he found her alive, but nearly unconscious, below her bed—whither she had crept when the castle was attacked.

By this time the sun had risen, and Norma Grant, which was the real name of Elspie, returned to Blackcraig as the acknowledged wife of Sir Patrick Dunbar. They only remained, however, at their castle, until Lucy was wed to the gallant young Laird of Auchinleck, and then he resigned the estate to his son, John, and retired into obscurity.

Phemie Colvil, the Laird of Ochiltree's daughter, and her mother, left the locality, and went to reside in Galloway. Some said Phemie was true to her first love; but as the *Auchinleck Manuscript* is silent on this subject, we cannot give it as a fact.

In conclusion, the Laird of Lochnoreis looked for a more eligible match than Phemie Colvil. Had her father fallen in honourable fight, instead of being hung like a common male-factor, he might have persisted in his suit; but he could not think of an alliance with a lady whose father had come through the hands of the hangman.

Sandy M'Phun deeply regretted having suggested the joke which terminated so fatally. He was often heard lamenting, when *tight*, to those who frequented the London Arms, that the bare sheep's head lost him two of his best customers on the water of Lugar.

THE CRUIVES OF CREE.

CHAPTER I.

THERE is something soothing and melodious in the voice of a mountain stream. All that is beautiful in nature loves to be near it. The birds sing sweeter, and the flowers bloom fairer on its banks than anywhere else—at least, so thought the Laird of Creeside, John M'Lurg, who inhabited a goodly mansion which stood on the south bank of the Cree many years ago. Whether he was a direct descendant of the loyal old lady who induced her two sons to swear fidelity to the great Robert Bruce, when an outcast, history sayeth not; but of the antiquity of his pedigree he could show as good proofs as the Laird of Buttonhole, who maintained, although a tailor, that he was descended from one of the three sons of Noah, but he was uncertain which of them it was.

Creeside, as Mr M'Lurg was familiarly called by his unsophisticated neighbours, was the only surviving son of a large family. His father had died some years previous to the opening of this tale, and left his mother and him in peaceful possession of the quaint old house and the acres attached to it. As mother and son had enough and to spare of worldly gear, John gave himself up to hunting and fishing, and many a pleasant hour was spent pursuing the latter pastime, of which he was extremely fond. It was while following this harmless occupation, along the Cree, that he first met Jessie Mackay, the young and beautiful heiress of Craigsmoor, and was smitten at once with her faultless beauty and fairy form. Whether by chance or premeditation, after the first meeting, Jessie found her way, almost daily, to the Cruives of Cree. The reason assigned by Jessie for this was, that she always found a world of enjoyment in the sough of falling waters, and that she thought the flowers on Mr M'Lurg's estate fairer than any she ever saw.

John felt flattered by this simple preference, and gradually there sprung up between them a close intimacy, which ended in John making a declaration of his love to Jessie, which she shyly admitted she reciprocated.

Great was the astonishment, therefore, of the inhabitants of Minnigaff when the banns were proclaimed. Indeed, it took the busybodies of the village completely by storm. Miss Tattler, the draper's daughter, declared, in a scornful manner, that it was a most unseemly match; that Creeside could be her father; that it was undutiful and heathenish to desert his old mother, now in her dotage, for any silly, sentimental, baby-faced creature: while Miss Gloomie shook her head ominously and said, 'naething but a judgment could follow such conduct.' Of course this undercurrent of clatter never reached the ears of John or Jessie; but there was one sitting in the ancient church, that peaceful Sabbath morning, that heard the proclamation with rage and disappointment. But he was a man of action, not words.

Peter M'Dowall, of Garfar, was a full cousin of Creeside, and had been led to believe, from his infancy, by his doating mother, that his rich relative would never marry, and that, as he was the only surviving relation, he was certain to become his heir. As year after year sped on, and Mr M'Lurg showed no decided preference for any of the belles of the parish, the expectations at Garfar became stronger and stronger as time wore on. Therefore, the announcement that Creeside was about to lead to the altar Jessie Mackay raised a mist before his eyes that obscured all the dreams of golden pieces and broad acres ever he had entertained.

He felt his senses reel where he was sitting, beside his wife, but being a consummate hypocrite, as worldly men generally are, he bowed his head, and held his throbbing brow with his hands, as if invoking a blessing on their union. What the text was, or what the minister said, Garfar heard not. But one intelligible sentence fell on his ear, during a sermon that he dreaded was never to end, and that was 'in conclusion, dear brethren.' Wiping the perspiration from his brow he hurried forth, and waited for Creeside among the memorials of the dead; but although he gazed on these grassy mounds, containing the ashes of old and young, with whom he had conversed while living, those sad remembrancers failed to touch a chord in his hard worldly heart. At last he saw Creeside issuing forth, and telling Peggy—the name by which he invariably called his wife—to smooth her wrinkled face, he advanced and shook his cousin warmly by the hand, exclaiming as he did so, ' I'm sure, Laird, this was a joyful surprise to me this morning.'

' I was telling my mother so before I left for the kirk that you were the only relative I had, and that I was sure you would rejoice ower my good fortune.'

' Rejoice, Laird, I'm delighted! but really I think ye micht hae taken me into yer confidence,' said Garfar, deprecatingly, retaining the smile on his bland face.

' I wanted, man, to keep the affair as quiet as possible, for as Jessie wisely observed, folks' faults were sure a' to be raked up when they were going to get married.'

' Very sensibly spoken, indeed. I'm sure when Peggy an' me were proclaimed the Cree wad hae scarcely stopped the mouths of the crones that spaed oor future misfortunes, and I'm sure, although we haena been blest wi' any bairns yet, there's no a happier pair on the Water o' Cree.' Garfar looked at his amiable spouse for a confirmation of this assertion, but Peggy, to avoid the scrutiny of his cunning grey eyes, pretended she was reading the inscription on a newly-raised tombstone, and the only response that reached the ear of Creeside from Peggy was a sigh. The fact is, if it was possible, she was more selfish and worldly than Garfar, but she was not such an adept at disguising her feelings. So bitterly did she feel the anticipated loss of Creeside that she could not have smiled, at that moment, for the wealth of the county of Wigtown.

As Creeside contrasted the long, lank figure of Peggy, arrayed in a grey gown, so narrow around the skirt, that he mentally wondered how she managed to walk in such a sack, with that of Jessie, who was standing at a little distance conversing with a friend, a scarcely perceptible smile flitted over his handsome face. As he took this momentary glance at Peggy's skinny neck and shrunken breasts, Garfar was watching him narrowly. Guessing what was passing through Creeside's mind, he felt a strong desire to strangle him where he stood, but with a violent effort he suppressed his passion, and with a blessing on his lips and a curse in his heart he bade his rich relation good-bye, and walked rapidly away, followed by his happy wife.

Creeside looked after them, with a smile on his face, until the trees hid them from his view, and then said, half aloud— ' Well, if Garfar and Peggy are the representatives of wedded bliss, I would be better with my respected mother than Jessie yet.'

Peggy, notwithstanding the want of cloth in the skirt of her gown, was not long in overtaking her loving spouse, and exclaimed, on coming up with him, ' Weel, of a' the hypocrites that ever crossed a kirk door, I'll swear ye're the warst.'

' If ye rouse me the day,' cried Garfar, turning savagely round on his better half, ' ye lang-legged limmer, after what I hae seen and heard, I'll douk ye in the Cree.'

' Try it, my bonny man, try it, Garfar,' cried Peggy, shaking her skinny hand in his face, ' and ye'll find it's no' the puir half-starved hind and his silly wife ye hae to deal wi'.'

Had not a turn in the pathway brought them suddenly in close proximity to a gipsy's encampment, it is uncertain how the dispute might have ended, but at this moment Garfar observed Gibb Armstrong, one of the most notorious reivers of the Borders, standing at the door of his tent; and admonishing Peggy to ' rin awa' hame an' get the kail ready, like a guid lass,' he bent his steps in the direction of the gipsy's camp, with anything but friendship in his heart towards Creeside.

CHAPTER II.

IN the days of which we write, county police were undreamed of; and as for public conveyances, there were none. The roads were always crowded with tramps of every description, but of pedlars, tinklers, and gipsies, there was an innumerable company. The first named class were made welcome in every house in the country, for in many villages there was no such a thing as a drapery establishment, selling goods at 15 or 20 per cent. below prime cost, to the great astonishment of Jock and the delight of Jenny when they now pay a visit to the town. The second were also in demand by many a frugal rustic, who could ill afford to buy a new pat or umbrella when they were cracked or injured; but the gipsies were more feared than loved or required. People wondered how they lived, for they followed no kind of useful occupation, yet they were merry and meatlike. Neither could they be charged by any around their encampment with theft; therefore, the lairds who had them located on their land felt quite at ease. Garfar was in the habit of taking some of his stock yearly to Carlisle, and had became acquainted with Armstrong under peculiar circumstances. One of the gipsy's gang was indicted to stand his trial at Carlisle for sheep stealing, and as Garfar was the only witness who could really hang him, as Gibb Armstrong observed when he called on him at the 'Angel Inn' the night previous to the trial, it was with infinite delight the gipsy chief learned, before he was long in conversation with Garfar, that he was an avaricious, unprincipled man, and that for a small sum of money he was willing to stand in the witness-box and prove the innocence of Johnstone; which he did, to the intense satisfaction of the whole gang, on the following day.

Ever afterwards there existed a seeming friendship between Garfar and Armstrong, and when the latter visited Wigtownshire he generally located himself on the laird's land.

'Here comes the greedy churl who saved ye frae the hempen cravat at Carlisle,' observed Armstrong, as he stood lounging at the tent door, to Johnstone inside.

'He's a precious scamp; but I'm far mistaken if his greed disna get him into a waur scrape than mine yet.'

'Hush, Johnstone, here he is.'

'Guid mornin' to ye, Mr Armstrong,' said Garfar, as he advanced with the usual smile on his face, and the same soft, low voice that he studied to assume upon all occasions, and held out his hand.

'Good morning, Garfar; I hope you and your amiable lady are well.'

This allusion of Armstrong's to Peggy's amiability made Garfar wince, but suppressing his ire he smilingly answered in the affirmative, and then asked if he could have a word with him privately.

'Oh! certainly, Laird, certainly. We have a spacious anteroom here,' answered Armstrong, as he glanced upwards at the cloudless sky and then at the limpid stream,—

'Ours the truly regal palace,
    Grander than the monarch's home;
Lovely earth its flowery carpet,
    Starry heaven its glittering dome.'

D

'Bless me! I didna imagine, Armstrong, ye dabbled in poetry,' exclaimed Garfar, as he slowly led the way to the side of the Cree.

'Neither I do, Garfar, but when I was younger and happier I was fond of it. What's your will wi' me?' As Armstrong asked this he seated himself on the trunk of a fallen tree, pulled out his pipe, struck a light, and commenced to smoke vigorously, keeping, however, his twinkling dark eyes on the face of the laird.

Garfar commenced his story by stating his relationship to Creeside, talked of his reputed wealth, and went on to state, that until to-day he had always calculated on becoming its inheritor.

'Ay,' interrupted Armstrong; 'and what has occurred to-day to blight your expectations?'

'He's gaun to marry a young bit lassie, the heiress o' Craigsmoor, like as he hadna enough already.'

'There's some folk never content,' observed the gipsy, philosophically, as he dreamily watched the smoke curling from his lips. 'But come to the point at once, man, I hate this beating about the bush; if I can safely serve you, I will, for auld langsyne.'

'Weel, in a word, Armstrong, wad ye take in hand to rid the country of Jessie Mackay for a guid filled purse o' gowd?'

'I suppose if I was to substitute world for country I would be reading your thoughts aright,' answered Armstrong, keeping his eyes bent on the ground, and drawing his hat further down on his brow.

'I'm no a man gien to murder, Armstrong, although if ye choose to dispose o' her that way, I'll no be speering ye ony impertinent questions.'

The gipsy shook the ashes from his pipe, rose slowly up, and turning his back to the laird, looked long and earnestly at the sunlit stream. Turning again to the laird he said, 'I have been thinking about your proposal, but you'll better go home and mature your plans. In my opinion your far ower hasty. This girl may never have a child. I suppose Peggy was a likely enough lady to bear a family when you married her, and it's more than probable she may never have a bairn to heir your wealth.'

'Oh, Armstrong,' cried the laird, excitedly, 'dinna speak o' my wealth; I'm poor, wretchedly poor.'

'Well, well, man, I want none of your gear. Believe me, it's time enough to move in this affair when your cousin has an heir born.'

'I daresay ye're right, Armstrong; but I was so exasperated this morning that I'm clean beside mysel'.'

'When ye think it ower ye'll find I'm right. Goodbye—dinner was ready when I left.' As the gipsy said this he turned and retraced his way to the tent, muttering as he went, 'The hell-hound wants me to commit murder to enrich him, but, thank God, I'm not that length yet.'

When he entered the tent he asked a young girl where Johnstone was, and was told that he slipped out immediately after him. Armstrong knit his brows, and sat down in silence to his dinner.

While vexation and envy raged in the hearts of Garfar and his wife, Creeside and Jessie were sunning themselves in each other's smiles. At last the happy day arrived which saw them united in the bonds of matrimony, and Garfar and his wife were both present on the joyous occasion. No one looking at the smil-- ing face of the laird could imagine there was a seed of bitterness in his heart, which was destined to produce fruit to poison the atmosphere of that happy home. But we must not anticipate.

Month followed month of unalloyed happiness at Creeside, and at last it became apparent, to the most superficial observer, that Mrs M'Lurg was in the happy state in which ladies like to be who love their lords.

Peggy was the first to observe her altered appearance, and with tears of vexation pointed it out to her more obtuse husband, who now resolved on a definite line of policy.

It was autumn, and Armstrong and his gang were again encamped on his land. Without speaking about his terrible project to Peggy, he took the foot-path leading to the 'gipsies' home;' and giving an urchin, who was gamboling along the Cree, a penny, he dispatched him for Johnstone, whom he saved from being hung at Carlisle. After his unsatisfactory confer-ence with Armstrong, he had been waited on by Johnstone, who had lurked among the bushes, and heard every word of the conversation that passed between them. At that time he offered to carry out Garfar's murderous design; but the laird had taken Armstrong's advice, and resolved to wait patiently until he saw what would occur, promising, however, that if he needed assistance he would give him the first chance of earning an honest penny. Johnstone, who was a hardened wretch, was constrained at the time to be content with this promise; but when the boy told him what the gentleman was like who wished to speak to him, he conjectured that Garfar had now a job for him, and hurried rapidly to the bank of the Cree, where he was sitting.   They held a long, whispered conversation, looking fearfully around them every moment. At last they struck their fearful bargain, and separated.   But we must reserve, for another chapter, the effects of their diabolical compact.

CHAPTER III.

IF the darkest hour is before day, ofttimes a joyous, bright morning is the precursor of a storm.   In this world of change, we know not what an hour may bring forth.   Our cup of happiness may be running over, but before we can raise it to our lips some unseen hand may dash it to the earth, and substitute for our joy—despair, agony, and death.

Creeside, when he arose the morning after the meeting between Garfar and Johnstone, was a happy man; happy in the love of his young beautiful wife; blest with the friendship and esteem of nearly all who knew him in the villages of Newton-Stewart and Minnigaff—we say *nearly*, for good men have sometimes great enemies. Having enough and to spare of gear, and being conscious of having wronged no man, he had in and around him all the elements of happiness.

After partaking of a hearty breakfast, he began to make his usual preparations for going to fish.   'This should be a guid morning for catching a few trout in the Cree,' he observed, as he continued busy arranging his fishing tackle; 'I see there has been a guid shower through the nicht.'

'Take my advice, John,' said old Mrs M'Lurg, as she hobbled into the kitchen, leaning on her staff, 'au' stay at hame to-day.'

'Hoots, mother, this is the best day for fishing we have had this last month; an' ye ken Jessie's found of a trout.'

'I'm no' that fond o' them, however, dear John, that I wad like ye to disobey grannie to procure them,' observed Jessie, with a winning smile.

'What reason hae ye for interdicting me this morning, mother?' asked John, rather pettishly.

A word from either Jessie or his mother would at any time have deterred him from going to the Galloway Arms, even supposing it would have deprived him of the company of Willie Blair, the saddler, who was reputed to be the best angler in Wigtownshire, but this was his favourite occupation, and he was nettled a little at his aged mother's interference.

'I'll tell ye my reason, but I ken ye'll laugh at me before I hae dune,' said his mother, as she seated herself on the settle-bed. 'Last nicht I dreamed '——

'I kent it wad be something o' that kind,' cried Creeside, interrupting her, good-naturedly.

'For shame, John! hear what your mother has got to say,' exclaimed Jessie, reprovingly.

'Weel, weel, bairns, maybe it's a' nonsense, but ye can listen to it for a' that,' observed the old lady, quietly.

'Oh! we'll manage to do that,' said John, laughingly, and continuing his preparations.

'I saw ye in my dream,' resumed his mother, 'standing on a tummock o' grass fishing abune the Cruives o' Cree. Everything around ye was smiling and beautiful, but suddenly there arose oot o' the lang, rank grass on the bank a huge snake. Rearing itsel' up on its tail, it watched ye eagerly; aye when ye turned aboot it hid itsel', and the moment ye began to fish it peered up again. Greatly to my astonishment and horror its face began to assume the lineaments o' Garfar's, and, watching its opportunity, it sprang suddenly forward and struck ye wi' its stang, just there.' As the old lady said this, she laid her withered hand on the back of her son's head. 'I saw ye stagger and fa'—not into the Cree, but into an abyss, sae deep au' misty that I couldna see the bottom. I tried my best to scream, but my tongue clove to the roof o' my mouth, syne I awoke trembling with fear.'

'The nichtmare, mother; naething else. What did ye take to supper last nicht?'

'I hope sae, John; but somehow I hae a strange presentiment that some great misfortune is aboot to happen.'

'Mother, ye shouldna talk in this gloomy manner, seeing the state Jessie's in,' urged John, as soon as he obtained an opportunity of doing so privately. 'Cheer up; I'll be hame by

noon for my dinner.' As Creeside said this he swung his basket
on his back, and, taking his rod in his hand, sallied forth.

As he passed the Cruives of Cree, a strange feeling came
over him, but this he attributed to hearing his mother's dream
before he left; therefore he tried to dismiss the thought with
busying himself unwinding his line, and beginning to fish up
the stream. The water was, as he surmised, in capital order,
and as he consigned trout after trout to the basket, everything
was forgotten in the excitement of the sport. At last he
reached a pool about two hundred yards above the Cruives,
and as the bank was thickly wooded, he had to approach its
very edge and stand on a grassy knoll or tummock—these are
common almost to every stream in Scotland. Stepping carefully lest it might give way beneath his weight, and precipi-
tate him head foremost into the 'weil,' not that he was afraid
of being drowned, as he was a capital swimmer, but the idea
of being wet was disagreeable. Having got himself fixed to
his mind, he commenced to whip the surface of the stream
very earnestly. 'Ha! a salmon, by George!' he exclaimed;
' but I hae missed it. Try again is no' forbidden.' Muttering
to himself in this manner, he applied himself with greater
assiduity to his task, and as he endeavoured to induce the fish
to rise again he was unconscious of everything around him.

As a tiger or beast of prey crawls through a jungle after its
victim, so did Johnstone, the gipsy, watch every movement of
Creeside. Whenever he changed his position, down went the
head of the wretch who was employed to murder him among
the brushwood and rank grass, which formed an impervious
screen between him and his victim. It may be thought strange
that Garfar selected his cousin and spared his wife, seeing that
she was about to become a mother; but he could reach Creeside with less danger, and his calculation was that the shock
occasioned by her husband's death would induce premature
parturition, and the whole family would be stricken down with
the one blow.

Crouchingly, Johnstone approached Creeside, and seeing
him standing in such a favourable position for his diabolical
purpose, and so intently bent on the sport, he drew from
beneath his coat a heavy bludgeon and advanced to within a
yard of his back. Creeside would in all probability have heard
the reptile breathing behind him, for his breath came thick and

pantingly, but at that very moment the salmon rose again, and
he exclaimed joyfully—'Hooked at last.'

That moment the gipsy raised his club and struck Creeside
a savage blow on the back of the head, and with a groan
he fell forward and disappeared in the pool; but, to the horror
of the murderer, he carried the fishing rod with him, firmly
clutched in his hand, and as the top of it protruded out of the
water several feet, he imagined that it pointed towards him
menacingly. Here was an unforeseen dilemma, a contingency
for which neither the gipsy nor Garfar had made any calculation, and as he could not swim, he fled from the spot, leaving
this tell-tale trace of the murder behind him.

CHAPTER IV.

WHILST the murderer was flying in the direction of Garfar, to
tell him the result of his morning's work, and demand his pay,
Willie Blair, a saddler from Newton-Stewart, arrived at the
'Cruives of Cree,' and being, as has been before remarked, a keen
angler, he unwound his line, and began his morning's favourite amusement. He was soon rewarded for his trouble by
hooking a large salmon, which dashed swiftly up the stream in
the direction of the pool where the lifeless body of Creeside
was lying. Willie expertly paid out the last yard of the line
off the reel, and then began to kill the fish, but this seemed a
very difficult task to accomplish. At last its efforts to escape
became languid, and Willie began the most exciting part of the
sport, endeavouring to land 'the monster,' as he called him.

Slowly he wore him towards the spot where he was standing, but in a moment he stopped hauling in his line, and stood
staring at the top of a fishing rod which protruded some feet
out of the water. 'Somebody has lost their wand this morning,' he soliloquised; 'an' feth it seems a guid ane, but it's
drifting this way.' Having arrived at this satisfactory conclusion, he landed his fish, but to his great astonishment
another line was entwined with his own. In a moment it was
suggested to his mind that the line belonged to the rod which
he saw above the water. The first thing he brought to the
bank was the large salmon which Creeside had hooked before he
received his death-blow from the gipsy. Carefully he laid it

beside the one he had caught, and then began to haul in the line.

'Surely there's something handing it,' he muttered, as the top of the rod disappeared when he laid a gentle strain on the line. 'It's impossible, hooever, there can be anither salmon on it.' With great patience and care he at last succeeded in catching the top of the rod, and drew it towards him, thinking from the great weight attached to it that it had got foul of the root of some tree which had lain long in the pool. The first thing which struck a chill to his heart was the hand of a man firmly grasping the rod, the next moment the ghastly features of Creeside rose to the surface, and with a cry of horror he fell backwards on the bank quite insensible.

In the meantime, Johnstone and Garfar were closeted together, haggling about the money the former was demanding for committing the murder.

'It's far ower muckle, Johnstone, for half an hour's wark. A hundred gold pieces! I doot ye maun be doing wi' the half o' it.'

'Hand ower the cash at ance, an' dinna stan' there shakin' a' mornin' wi't in yer han', for not a farthing less will I tak'.'

'If ye're sure he's deid, there's the siller; but it's far ower muckle.' Saying this, Garfar handed the wretch his blood money.

Placing the bag containing the gold in his bosom, Johnstone said, with a hideous grin, 'I doot the murder will sune be discovered.'

'Ha!' exclaimed Garfar savagely, as he clutched the gipsy by the breast, where he had deposited the money, 'If ye hae deceived me I'll hae yer life on the spot whaur ye stand.'

'Let go yer grip, ye auld savage, or I'll slit your weasand.'

As Garfar saw the blade of a knife glittering before his eyes, he relinquished his grip, and cried pantingly, 'Tell me what ye mean.'

'Creeside's in the Miller's Weir, but when I struck him he held a firm grip o' his fishing rod, and took it alang wi' him into the hole, whaur it may be seen bobbing abune the water.'

'Compose yersel', Johnstone, an' come alang wi' me, I maun see what it is like. Maybe ye can get a grip o' it when I'm alang wi' ye.'

'I'll no try.'

'Weel, weel, come wi' me, and I'll try.'

Leaving the room where this conference was held, the two villains sauntered leisurely along the Cree until they came in sight of Willie Blair, who was in the act of dragging the fishing rod towards him. Crouching down behind a tree they observed the head of Creeside raised above the water, and heard Blair's cry as he fell insensible on the bank.

'Come on, quick, Johnstone,' cried Garfar, in a suppressed voice, 'we'll charge Blair wi' the murder. We can easily swear we saw them quarrelling aboot the fish—come on.'

The gipsy, as he hurried after him, had an indistinct notion that Garfar was about to charge Blair with the murder of his friend, and the very thought lifted an immense weight off his heart.'

'Villain! what's this ye hae been aboot this mornin'?' cried Garfar, as he collared the scarcely conscious Mr Blair.

'What dae ye mean, Garfar?' asked Blair, first looking at the one and then at the other as they stood over him.

'Hearken to his brazen-faced effrontery,' exclaimed Garfar, in a mocking voice. 'Did the gipsy and me no see you strike Creeside on the heid and hurl him into the pool, no ten minutes since.'

'It's a lie! a damnable falsehood!' cried Blair, springing to his feet, and casting Garfar from him with such a force that he fell heavily to the earth.

'I take you to witness, Johnstone, that the villain wants to murder me as he did my friend.'

' I'm no gaun to bandy words wi' ye and yer thievish looking comrade, but if ye hae a spark o' humanity remaining in ye, help me to carry hame the body o' my dear cronie."

'Hearken the hypocritical loon,' exclaimed Garfar, sneeringly. 'On him, Johnstone, lest he escapes.' Garfar was in the act of rushing again on Blair, when a powerful hand was laid on his shoulder, and Armstrong, the gipsy chief, demanded in a stern tone, as he pointed to the lifeless form of Creeside, 'Who did this?'

'There stands the murderer,' answered Garfar, as he pointed malignantly at Blair.

'It's as base a lie as ever was uttered by the mouth of man, believe me, sir. I know no more of this foul deed than the babe at its mother's breast.'

'I do believe you.' said Armstrong, emphatically.

'Johnstone, do you know anything of this foul deed?' asked his comrade, turning suddenly round on him.

'How should I know about it?' asked Johnstone in a voice that might be tremulous with passion or guilt.

'That's not answering my question, but asking one,' observed Armstrong.

'Garfar, I need not ask you anything about the murder, you're too respectable a man to know anything of a deed of this kind.' The gipsy said this in a voice of scorn that sounded strangely in the ears of Blair.

'Curse ye for a wanderin' thief, hoo daur ye insinuate that I ken anything aboot a crime o' this kind.'

'I could point to a man that's worse than a thief; but bear a hand and help me, Mr Blair, home with the corpse of Mr M'Lurg to Creeside. A sad sight it will be for his young bonny wife.' As the gipsy said this he bent over the murdered man, and raised him up in his powerful arms.

'Johnstone, what are ye afraid of?' shouted Armstrong; 'are ye no gaun to gie us a hand?'

'I'll no pit a han' to him to-day,' cried Johnstone, as he turned away with a shudder from the face of Creeside, whose eyes he imagined to be fixed menacingly upon him. Garfar also refused to assist, but said he would hurry on and break the sad news to his auld mother, and poor wife, as gently as possible.

CHAPTER V.

So unfeelingly had Garfar announced the death of Creeside to his young wife and aged mother that, by the time the gipsy Armstrong and Willie Blair had reached the house, with the Laird's body, Mrs M'Lurg's life was despaired of. She was passionately fond of her husband, and the rude manner in which Garfar declared he had been murdered by his friend and cronie, Willie Blair, had stricken her down at once. One fainting fit had succeeded another, in rapid succession, since she had heard the news, so that by the time Creeside's body was laid in the hall, she was quite unconscious. But his mother, to every appearance, was calm and collected. Seventy summers had passed over her head, and during their flight she had encountered many a gust of adverse fortune. True, she had never met anything like this, but in the ever-changing scenes of human life she had learned patience and Christian resignation. Having despatched a servant for Dr Grey, she ordered Garfar from the room, and used all the means in her power to restore Jessie to consciousness.

No sooner had the servant alighted from his horse, at the Doctor's door, than he was surrounded by a crowd of people inquiring what was the matter at Creeside.

'Willie Blair has murdered my master,' was all he had time to communicate, when the door was opened, and he hurried inside to tell Dr Grey his errand.

'Blair has murdered Creeside!' flew from door to door with the rapidity of lightning, through Minnigaff and Newton-Stewart.

At last the sad news was communicated to Mary Dill, Willie Blair's sweetheart, by Nellie Glen. 'I canna believe it, nor I wunna believe it!' cried Mary, as, springing to her feet, and casting her sewing aside, she wrapped her plaid around her and started for the scene of the murder, notwithstanding the expostulations of her mother to the contrary.

The way to Creeside was now crowded with old and young, for never since the murder of the Laird of Crosbie, some fifty years ago, had anything like this occurred in the neighbourhood.

By the time Miss Dill reached Creeside Mrs M'Lurg had been delivered of a son ; and as Garfar maintained that he saw Willie Blair commit the murder, Dr Grey, who was a Justice of the Peace, ordered him to be conveyed to Wigtown immediately.

'Tell me, Willie! in mercy tell me, if ye are innocent o' this foul crime!' exclaimed Mary Dill, as she forced her way through the crowd by which she was surrounded, with tears streaming down her youthful face.

'Be calm, dearest Mary,' said Blair, in as cheerful a voice as he could command. 'Although circumstances are against me, I'm as innocent o' the death o' Creeside as ye are.'

'Oh, thank God for this assurance,' cried Mary, drying her tears. 'I feel confident this is the truth.'

'Ye feel confident,' sneered Garfar unfeelingly. 'An' muckle yer faith in his innocence wull dae tae save him. Tak' my advice and awa' hame like a bonny lassie, and mind yer ain affairs. Did I not see him murder my dear cousin?'

' An' is it on yer evidence they're gaun to commit Mr Blair
to jail?' cried Mary, turning on him fiercely. ' Ye miserly
auld hunks, I wudna be the least surprised if it wad turn oot ye
had a hand in his death yersel.'

' Nor I cither,' whispered Armstrong, the gipsy, in her ear.

Mary started, and looked wildly in the stranger's face, but
placing his finger on his lip, he shook his head, enjoining silence.

The crowd hovered about until they saw Willie Blair bound
hand and foot and thrown into a cart in charge of two con-
stables, and then dispersed in various directions, discussing as
they went along the guilt or innocence of the saddler.

Garfar pled hard with the doctor to see dear Jessie and the
bairn before he left, but Dr Grey said it was impossible in the
present state of Mrs M'Lurg, and he was forced to depart
without his evil eye resting on the fragile widow, whose joyous
life his villany had so ruthlessly crushed. Praying that he
might never see her again in life, he left Creeside, and reached
home in the afternoon, but the news of Creeside's murder had
preceded him.

' This is a fearfu' job,' began Peggy, as soon as he entered;
' an' hoo strange ye should be the one that saw the crime committed ? '

Peggy was hard, worldly, and unkind, but much as she
coveted the fair domain of Creeside, she never dreamed of
perpetrating such a deed to obtain possession of it.

' Ay, it's a fearfu' affair,' answered the laird moodily, ' but
there's never a great lose but there's some sma' profit; Mrs
M'Lurg is safely delivered of a son and heir.'

' Then that's an end to our prospects of ever getting Creeside,' observed Peggy despondingly.

' I dinna ken; the bairn micht dee, an' as Creeside has
made nae wull, the property wad be oors in spite o' the deil.'

' Ye forget his mother.'

' I forget naething aboot her; but she's seventy years o'
age, an' she canna live much langer.'

' That's very true!" said Peggy, brightening up a little.
' Are ye for nae dinner to-day ?'

' No.'

' Puir man! ye have been sadly put aboot this morning,'
said Peggy, in such an affectionate tone, that the laird
rewarded her, not with a kiss, but by springing to his feet and

exclaiming—'What cursed nonsense is this!' The next moment he was gone.

Peggy, however, consoled herself by stroking the cat affectionately; plainly proving that we must have some creature on which to lavish our love; but if some of the aspirants for heaven, who go along the streets caressing poodle dogs, cleanly washed and adorned with ribbons, were to adopt some of the dirty, naked, houseless children that swarm on our streets, they would be nearer the mark.

Armstrong, before leaving Creeside, watched his opportunity of speaking to Miss Dill privately, and told her to keep up her heart, as he was sure of Blair's innocence.

'Then what was the reason you did not tell them sae before he was sent to Wigtown?' cried Mary, again bursting into tears.

'You told them so, but it had little effect.'

'That's true,' said Mary, heaving a deep sigh.

'Your a brave lass, and I liked the spirit ye showed Garfar; sae to extricate yer lover oot o' this scrape, I'll dae what I can; but if I'm to assist him, you must mention to no one that ye were speaking to Armstrong, the gipsy.'

'Armstrong, the gipsy,' reiterated Mary. 'Oh! in mercy tell me if ye ken anything aboot it.'

'Nothing, properly speaking, nothing; but I may tell you in confidence that I discovered this morning a clue which, with my experience, may guide me to put the saddle on the richt horse.'

'When wull I hear frae ye or see ye again?' asked Mary, looking up at his face imploringly.

'If ye're not afraid o' ghaists, meet me this evening about six o'clock in the kirkyard o' Minnigaff.'

'I'll be sure to be there, and noo, gudebye till then. Heaven grant ye may be successful in unravelling this foul mystery.'

'Goodbye, and cheer up, I'll dae all I can.' As he said this he walked rapidly away along the Cree.'

On he went until he reached an oak tree which grew beside the pathway, when he stooped down and lifted something from among the rank grass, which he instantly consigned to a capacious inside pocket of his coat. Smiling grimly, he hurriedly pursued his way until he reached the encampment. Entering his tent, he sent for Johnstone.

'Well, Johnstone, I have sent for you to ask you a question or two privately, so you'll better squat yoursel' doon and hear what I have got to say. In the first place, whaur were ye this morning?' asked Armstrong, fixing his eyes keenly on the face of his comrade.

'I'm not in a humour to gratify your curiosity,' answered the villain, sulkily.

'Ah! ha, my brave comrade; but I want an answer, and I'm determined to have it.'

'It seemed to me this morning ye were anxious to place me and Garfar in a fix doon at Creeside.'

'I doot ye hae *baith* placed yersels in a fix which ye will hae some difficulty o' extricating yersels oot o', notwithstanding the cunning o' yer employer; but, in a word, Johnstone, hoo muckle did Garfar gie ye for knocking Creeside into the pool?'

Johnstone started to his feet as if he had been stung by an adder. His face became of an ashy hue; the blood forsook his lips, and he trembled in every joint; he essayed to speak, but the words died in a hollow murmur on his parched lips; involuntarily he clutched the handle of his knife, but at this moment Armstrong drew from his inside pocket the article which he had lifted from the root of the oak tree, and held it up before him—it was a bludgeon covered with hair and blood.

'Spare me! ah, spare me! and I will tell you all,' cried the wretch, sinking at Armstrong's feet.

CHAPTER VI.

DURING the afternoon work was all but suspended in the villages of Newton-Stewart and Minnigaff. Groups of eager disputants were assembled here and there, discussing the all-absorbing theme—Creeside's murder. Those who knew Willie Blair best, affirmed that he was incapable of committing such a crime, no matter what amount of provocation he might receive. Then he was well known to be a man of the most kindly nature, and often known to neglect his business to promote the welfare and happiness of others. It was true he liked a song and a dram occasionally; and Misses Tattler and Gloomie maintained he had mair lasses than Mary Dill; but the latter failing—if true—was graciously forgiven by the majority of the ladies in the parishes around.

Those and similar arguments were brought forward by his friends—and they were numerous—but there was another class who argued that all the circumstances were against him. Creeside had left home after breakfast-time; so had Blair. Both their fishing rods were found lying together on the bank; and when Garfar and the gipsy first saw Blair, he was in the act of dragging his friend—as some folk were pleased to call him—out of the water.

'An' a friendly act it was,' observed Ross, the banker. 'Dae ye think that if Blair had killed him, and thrown him in the Cree, he wad hae waited to drag him oot again? Garfar and the gipsy may swear what they like, but if I was on the jury, I wadna credit their evidence.'

'The thing's unco improbable looking,' observed John Blair, the shoemaker; 'but if Garfar and Johnstone swear that they saw him strike the fatal blow, and throw him into the water, he'll swing for it. Although I could perceive frae look and manner o' Armstrong the gipsy, that he held the same opinion as Mr Ross; an', if I was to hazard an opinion, Garfar's the only interested person, that I ken o' in this neighbourhood, in the death o' Creeside.'

'An' we a' ken,' chimed in William Strachan, the publican, 'that he's a real Nabal. I'm sure, although he pits up his beast wi' me, he hisna bocht a gill this twelve months and mair.'

'Oh! I hae nae fault to find wi' Garfar for that,' observed Mr Blair, dryly, who, although living long anterior to the reign of teetotalers and Good Templars, had invariably observed that the people who frequented the public-house were the worst patrons of the shoeshop.

As the publican and shoemaker here went off at a tangent from the subject interesting to the reader, we will leave them to discuss the knotty problem, and follow Miss Dill to the old kirkyard of Minnigaff.

It was a bright September evening, and as Mary seated herself on a fallen tombstone, in the shadow of the church, her eyes wandered up the valley of the Cree, until its silvery windings were lost amidst the silence and solitude of the distant mountains. But although her eyes wandered over the enchanting panorama of hill and dale spread out before her, it yielded her no pleasure. If anything, it added to the poignancy of her grief, by reminding her of the happy hours she had spent, on the banks of the Cree, with her first and only lover. So sad were the recollections conjured up by the scenes around her, that she wrung her hands in mental agony, and burst into tears.

'Dry yer een, my bonnie bird,' said Armstrong, tapping her gently on the shoulder, ' ye hae no occasion to be weeping.'

' What a start ye gien me !' exclaimed Mary, springing to her feet, and smiling through her tears. ' I declare, I never heard ye approaching.'

' Oh ! I can believe that. Ye were ower busy tormenting yersel'—but sit doon, an' compose yer mind, I have news for ye.'

' Guid or bad?' asked Mary, looking wistfully in his face, as she drew her plaid closely around her, and reseated herself.

' If I was to say the news were good, na doot, the first thing ye wad dae, when ye went into the toon, wad be to proclaim it far an' near, an' very likely the name o' the man wha told ye. Noo I maun hae yer solemn promise before I say muckle mair, that let the news which I bring be good or bad, ye will keep them to yersel'. Recollect Blair's safety depends on your discretion.'

' Oh ! sir,' exclaimed Mary, eagerly, ' I'll swear a solemn aith if ye require it, that, even to my dear mother, wha is nearly as much put aboot as mysel', I will never mention it.'

' I dinna require an oath, your word is quite sufficient, when ye know yer lover's life depends on you an' me.'

' Is he guilty or innocent? tell me that, for, oh, I'm in an awfu' state of suspense.'

' He's as innocent as ye are.'

' Thank God for this assurance !' exclaimed Mary, devotedly clasping her hands together, and raising her eyes to heaven.

' Oh ! sir, if ye kent the weight o' sorrow an' uncertainty ye hae lifted off my heart, it should mak' ye happy.'

' Dinna greet ony mair, like a guid lass,' said Armstrong, soothingly.

' I'm that overjoyed,' cried Mary, sobbing and drying her tears, ' that I canna help it.'

' Ay, but tears will no' get yer lad oot o' Wigtown jail.'

' I thought ye said jist noo he was innocent,' said Mary, staring at the gipsy strangely.

'So I did. But many a time an innocent man has been hung, when the guilty escaped; an' had it no' been for a triffling discovery I made this morning, such wad hae been the fate o' Willie Blair, for Garfar an'—I'm ashamed to say it—yin o' my gang is willing, and will swear that they saw him commit the murder.'

'They maun be horrid wretches,' cried Mary, holding up her hands in astonishment; 'but it's maybe impertinent in me speerin'—dae ye ken the murderer?'

'Brawly noo, but I wasna richt sure when I saw ye last, although I strongly suspected wha it was.'

'An' are ye no gaun to denounce the wretch, and get Willie oot o' jail?'

'My evidence as yet is unsupported, an' one o' the men connected wi' the murder is rich an' influential, whereas, ye maun bear in mind that I'm only a gipsy. However, gang hame an' sleep soun, for I think I'll manage to clear Mr Blair. This is a' that I can tell ye at present.'

'I hope, sir, God will reward you for your kindness to me.'

'I hope sae,' observed the gipsy with a sigh. 'In the meantime, I maun bid ye guid nicht, for I hae anither party to see before I sleep.'

'When will I hear from you again?' asked Mary, holding out her hand.

'To-morrow, unless something extraordinary occurs, at the same hour. Remember yer promise. Good evening.' As the gipsy said this, he walked rapidly away in the direction of Garfar; Mary left the kirkyard with a lighter heart than she entered it.

While the foregoing interview was taking place between Miss Dill and the gipsy, Garfar and his amiable spouse were holding a *tete-a-tete* anent the young widow—Mrs M'Lurg, and her son.

'Is there nae appearance o' her deein, Peggy?' said Garfar, in a bitter tone.

'Nane that I could perceive,' answered Peggy, shaking her head; 'an' Dr Grey tauld me that the baby and her were progressing as favourable as could be expected, under the circumstances.'

'Did ye see the auld wife?'

'Ou ay; but she scarcely spoke to me.'

E

'Curse the hale pack o' them, but I'll hae Creeside yet, or it will be strange.'

'If the bairn lives that's impossible.'

'But it will die, an' that before lang,' cried Garfar, fiercely. 'Ever sin' I was a boy, I was taught to look upon mysel' as the heir o' Creeside, an' I'll be possessed o' it yet, in spite o' a' the brats that ever was born.'

A loud rap at the door interrupted the conversation, and when it was opened, to the great astonishment of Garfar, Armstrong stepped inside.

CHAPTER VII.

ALTHOUGH Armstrong's ideas of *meum et tuum* were very lax, yet he had a natural aversion to anything that savoured of cruelty. He had been a participator in many an unlawful act, but the very mention of murder made him quiver, therefore he looked upon the deed committed by Johnstone and Garfar with horror and loathing. From the former he had learned ample details of the crime, and been offered a share of the money received from Garfar for committing it, but he refused even to take the bag in his hand containing it. Towards the evening Johnstone had disappeared, and as Armstrong suspected him of being lurking somewhere in the neighbourhood for the purpose of either killing or carrying off the newly born heir to Creeside, he thought he would pay a visit to Garfar, and, by assuming a complete knowledge of the whole affair, endeavour to ascertain whether his fears were real or groundless.

Armstrong was no scholar, but he had learned a vast amount of knowledge during his wandering, predatory life. As chief of a band of gipsies, he well knew that if the murder of Creeside was traced to one of his gang, it would be hard to convince the Sheriff of Wigtownshire or the public that he was ignorant of the crime. Garfar he knew by former experience to be mean, selfish, and cruel, and, above all he ever knew, cunning. Therefore, it behoved him, if he wished to save his neck, not only to take energetic measures to frustrate the villains, but to feel his way with the utmost circumspection and prudence.

' Come awa', Armstrong,' said Garfar, as the gipsy entered,
' I was jist thinking aboot ye a minute ago.'

Armstrong knew this to be a falsehood to start with, but
having a particular line of policy chalked out for himself, he
thanked him and took the seat indicated.

Seeing that Peggy had left them, to look after the
beasts, Armstrong abruptly asked—' Whaur's Johnstone the
nicht ?'

' Hoo should I ken ?' asked Garfar, moving uneasily in his
chair.

' Oh ! I thocht as he had been working for you lately, ye
wad maybe ken.'

' Working for me ?' reiterated Garfar, as he arose from his
seat in evident alarm.

'Sit doon, and compose yersel',' said Armstrong, in a low
voice, ' for although I ken a' aboot it, I'm no gaun to inform
on ye.'

'Hush ! for Gude's sake, speak low. What dae ye ken ?'

' That ye gien Johnstone a hunner golden pieces to pit
Creeside into the Miller's Weil, and that he's awa noo to pit
the heir oot o' the road. I think ye micht hae gien an auld,
tried frien' like me a share o' the spoil.' All this was said by
Armstrong in a low whisper, while Garfar sat trembling like
an aspen leaf until he heard the concluding sentence, and then
he breathed easier.

' If I had thocht, Mr Armstrong, that ye wad hae taen
the job in haun, I wad hae employed nae ither body ; but I'll
tell you what you can dae for me, if Johnstone manages to
win in safely to Creeside the nicht, ye can swear, that's if I'm
suspected, that ye saw me sitting at my ain fire-end, and I can
also prove that I was at hame when Creeside was murdered
this morning—whisht, here's Peggy coming, I'll pay ye
again.'

As Peggy entered, he rose to his feet, and said in a loud
voice, ' I'll no gang oot the nicht, Armstrong—Gude nicht.'

Without deigning to reply, Armstrong hurried forth, mentally cursing Garfar. ' He'll no gang oot the nicht. He made
sure o' Peggy an' his red-legged maid o' the byre hearing that,'
cried Armstrong, foaming with passion, as he flew rather than
walked to Creeside. ' I can swear that I saw him sitting at
his ain fire-end if Johnstone is apprehended—as he will be as

sure as my name's Armstrong. I keut the auld fox wad secure himsel'. Noo, if I had laid an information against him, wad I not hae cut a fine figure. Armstrong's word, in a coort o' law, against the evidence o' the Laird o' Garfar! And what will his bonnie wife an' servant think but I was wanting him oot before they cam' in, and if my comrade got into trouble, it wad be quite a simple thing to swing Armstrong and him thegither. Ha! ha! Garfar, I learned my trade better on the borders than that comes to.'

It was wearing late when he arrived at Creeside, and a death-like stillness reigned in and around the house. In one apartment lay the lifeless body of Creeside, while in an adjoining room lay the young mother, hovering on the confines of eternity, for Dr Grey was very doubtful of her recovery. Of course, the baby was entrusted to the care of a skilful nurse, called Mary Cameron, whom the doctor had brought from Newton-Stewart. Mary and the infant had retired to a bed-room overlooking the Cree, and as it was now ten o'clock they had gone to rest. Perceiving from the light in the kitchen that the servants had not retired for the night, he approached it cautiously and listened to the conversation a moment before rapping. The theme of their talk was the murder, and as Rob Carson, the servant who went for the doctor, described the appearance minutely of his master when he was lying on the bank of the Cree, the rest of the servants, male and female, huddled closer together, and spoke in hollow whispers, as if afraid of their own voices.

'Dae ye think Dr Grey will stay a' nicht?' asked Jenny Forsyth at the hero of the party, Rob Carson.

'Nae doot o' that,' answered Rob; 'he'll be weel paid for't, let wha like live or die.'

Jenny declared she was glad o' that.

'What are ye glad o' that for? I'm sure, as far as I'm concerned, I could sleep in the same room wi' Creeside a'—— Lord, wha's that at the door!' exclaimed Rob, speaking as if he had the ague.

'Jenny, rin' like a guid lass, and see wha's dunnerin' at the door at this time o' nicht,' said Rob, in a supplicating tone.

'Na, I'm blest if I dae onything o' the kind; gang yersel' sin' ye're sic a brave man.'

Armstrong began to think that it was useless rapping again, so he lifted the latch and walked in.

'Oh, it's only Mr Armstrong!' exclaimed Rob, regaining his courage. 'Lord, if I had kent it was you, I wadna hae hesitated a minute.'

'Wha did ye think it was?' asked the gipsy, looking round him; but not seeing the man he wanted, he asked if Carmichael was about.

'He's in the stable.'

'I wish to speak wi' him; gude nicht.'

'They're awfu' queer folk thae gipsies,' observed Rob, gravely, as soon as the door was shut. 'I wadna gang wanderin' aboot at nicht as they dae for ony amount o' siller. I wunner what he'll be wanting wi' Carmichael.'

About ten minutes after the gipsy had left the kitchen, Carmichael entered it, and told them to draw down the blind of the window, and keep as quiet as mice until he came back again, supposing that to be an hour or two.

'What's in the wun noo?' asked Rob, who, if not extra brave, was very curious.

'I'll tell ye a' aboot it before ye sleep;' as Carmichael said this he rejoined Armstrong, who was waiting for him outside.

'We're gaun to hae a storm,' observed the gipsy. 'Is there any place we can shelter in aboot the garden?'

'Ay, there's a kind o' a simmer hoose convenient to the sleeping apartment o' the nurse; we can shelter there.'

'Come on fast, then, for it's raining in earnest.'

Scarcely had they ensconsed themselves in the arbour referred to when a brilliant flash of lightning illumined every object in the garden, which ran from the back of the house to the side of the Cree. The vivid flash of lightning was followed by a terrific peal of thunder, and down came the rain in torrents. Gradually the storm increased in violence, and before a quarter of an hour Carmichael and the gipsy were drenched to the skin.

'He'll hardly attempt it to-night,' whispered Carmichael.

'The very nicht for sic a job; whist, he's at the window!' exclaimed Armstrong, as a vivid flash of lightning revealed every object around them for a moment, and then all was dark as midnight—the hour it was.

CHAPTER VIII.

WHILE the gipsy and Carmichael were watching for the murderer in the garden, Dr Grey was attending to Mrs M'Lurg. Having administered to her a soothing opiate, she gradually fell into a calm sleep, and the Doctor, leaving a trusty servant at her bedside, retired to partake of some refreshment, of which he stood greatly in need. His supper being over, he threw himself back on the easy chair, and fell into a reverie concerning Creeside's murder, and its probable cause; but the more he thought about it, the greater became his perplexity. Johnstone and Garfar being the men who saw the murder committed he thought strange, because the latter was the only man who was likely to derive any benefit from his death. As Grey had been many years in the district, the character which Garfar bore for meanness, greed, and cunning was no secret to him; but hard and worldly as he knew him to be, it was difficult to believe him capable of committing such a horrid crime. With these thoughts floating through his mind, he dropped over asleep.

Wondering and wearying the servants sat huddled together, listening to the roar of the thunder and the heavy plashing of the rain. When they spoke at all it was in whispers, and it was only to express their astonishment at Carmichael's absence that ever the silence of the apartment was broken. Suddenly the loud report of a pistol broke the silence of midnight, making the females scream, and Rob Forsyth shake in his shoes, as he falteringly exclaimed, 'Lord save us a', what can that be?'

The shot which had alarmed the servants had also aroused the Doctor from his nap, and rushing into the kitchen he ordered Forsyth to accompany him to the back of the house, as he feared there was strange work going on there. As Rob appeared to hesitate, the Doctor was in the act of going alone, when the door was thrown open, and Armstrong and Carmichael entered, dragging the apparently lifeless form of Johnstone along with them.

'In God's name, men, what is the meaning of this horrid work? Who is this? or what has he been doing?' asked the Doctor, in great agitation.

'There lies the murderer of Creeside,' said Armstrong, pointing to the bleeding form lying on the floor.

'And he was within an ace of killing the wean that was born this morning,' added Carmichael, 'but oor frien' here cut short his career.'

Johnstone gave a convulsive quiver, and a faint groan, and the Doctor having caused his coat and vest to be taken off, examined the nature of the wound, which he pronounced at once to be fatal. Causing Johnstone's head to be raised a little, the Doctor forced a stimulant into his mouth, which had the effect of making the wretch open his eyes, and stare vacantly around him.

'Water, give me water,' murmured the dying man.

Complying with his request, the Doctor knelt down beside him and asked him who had employed him to murder Creeside.

'It was Garfar! Curse him! Where's the gold he gave me?' As he muttered these words, he clutched at his breast, from which the blood was profusely flowing, and fell back dead.

'This is awful!' exclaimed the Doctor, rising up and looking to Armstrong for an explanation of the tragic occurrences of the day and night.

Armstrong began and briefly narrated what the reader already knows—how that Garfar waited upon him on the day on which the banns were proclaimed between Mr M'Lurg and Jessie, offering him a sum of money if he agreed to destroy the life of the youthful bride, an offer which he scornfully refused; that when he heard of Creeside's murder in the morning he naturally suspected Garfar, but had no idea that one of his gang was mixed up in it until he found a club, belonging to the man lying there, covered with blood; but as our readers already know all that he rehearsed to the Doctor, we need not weary them with the repetition.

'Armstrong,' said the Doctor, 'I depend on you having the corpse of this miscreant removed as soon as possible. You must be aware that the existence of the dear young lady upstairs trembles between life and death; and,' he continued, turning to the servants, who stood trembling around, 'if any of you are so imprudent as to alarm your mistress by telling her of this terrible affair, you will be the cause of her death; so, beware. I will now go up and see how Mrs M'Lurg is doing, and then I will accompany you to the Garfar, for M'Dowall must not escape.'

As soon as the Doctor retired, Armstrong and Carmichael removed the body of Johnstone to the stable.

'The Doctor needna threaten me,' said Rob Forsyth, as soon as he found himself alone with the girls, ' for I wadna stop here after what has occurred if they would mak a prince o' me.'

'Which they are very unlikely to do,' dryly observed Jenny.

' Ye needna taunt me, my leddy, for if ye wad speak the truth, ye're jist as scared o' deid folk as I am.'

' I'm no' the least afeerd o' deid folk; my certes, it's the livin' anes that frichtens me. But ye may gang whaur ye like and when yo like, Rob, for tae speak plainly I wadna be named wi' a lad that was flied o' a bogle.'

How much more Jenny might have told of her mind is uncertain, for the Doctor's entrance cut short the altercation.

Day was breaking as the Doctor, Armstrong, and Carmichael sallied forth for the Garfar. The storm had subsided, but the Cree was running from bank to brae as they hurried along, determined to capture Garfar at all hazards. Leaving them on their way, let us hasten on before them and see what the Laird is doing.

Hour after hour Garfar had sat in his room waiting Johnstone's return, but when day began to break and there was no appearance of him, he experienced that mental agony known only to the guilty, and which it is impossible to describe. Throughout the silent watches of the night he had applied often to the bottle, so that at last he was neither waking nor sleeping, but in a kind of mental stupor, from which he was rudely startled by a loud knocking at the door.

' It canna be Johnstone,' he muttered, ' for he kens o' the back door being left open for him;' as he said this he arose, went to the window, and gazed out into the court. It was yet scarcely clear, but through the grey mist of the calm September morning he distinguished the forms of Messrs Grey, Armstrong, and Carmichael. 'It's a' up wi' me!' he cried, as he fled from the window and made for the back door as fast as his unsteady legs would carry him. But the gipsy had seen him at the window, and judging from his sudden disappearance he meant to effect his escape, he cried to the Doctor and Carmichael to guard the front door, while he hurried round, as quickly as he could, to the rear of the house.

This, however, was a matter of some difficulty, and before Armstrong had opened gates and waded through filth, fully five minutes had elapsed before he reached the rear of the house, giving, therefore, Garfar a fair start. Armstrong, however, saw him flying in the direction of the Cree, and being swifter, by far, of foot, he soon got within hailing distance.

'Stop, ye murdering loon! stop,' shouted Armstrong at the top of his voice, but this made Garfar redouble his speed. On fled the Laird, regardless of bush and brake, until he reached the ford, which he had often crossed when there was as strong a spate, and as he could now hear the gipsy's footsteps rapidly approaching, without a moment's reflection he dashed into the stream. But the mental anxiety through which he had passed during the night, and his frequent demands on the bottle, unfitted him for encountering successfully the force of the stream, and before he had proceeded many yards he was swept off his feet and borne like a bubble on the surface of the rapid current. With one wild shriek he sank beneath the impetuous water, and the next moment all was still.

Armstrong turned away from the bank of the Cree with a shudder, and as he did so he vowed to amend his life, a resolution which he kept. He found the Doctor and Carmichael anxiously awaiting his return, to whom he briefly related Garfar's lamentable end.

Before the conclusion of the day, Willie Blair, the saddler, was restored to his friends; and if the parting between him and Mary was a sad one, the reader can imagine with what joy she welcomed him home, with an untarnished name. A short time afterwards they were united in marriage, and Mary never saw him go to the Cree to fish but she remembered the fearful crime with which he was charged.

The bonnie widow of Creeside, as she was invariably called in the neighbourhood, gradually recovered her health, but never her youthful buoyancy of spirits. She lived to see her son's children romping around her on the banks of the Cree.

Old Mrs M'Lurg did not long survive her son's death, but was quietly laid beside her forefathers in the ancient kirkyard of Minnigaff.

Peggy, owing to her husband dying without making a will, was forced to leave the Garfar, and as the son born to Creeside became its owner, Armstrong was put in possession as overseer, the duties of which he faithfully discharged until his death, which did not occur for many years after the death of Garfar.

   .   .   .   .

Our tale is now told, and the moral of it may be found in the words of the great Apostle Paul—'The love of money is the root of all evil.'   This is the greatest sin of the nineteenth century. Men toil, cheat, and murder to obtain it, and after all, it yields no happiness.   We have seen lumpers on the quays stagger beneath loads of silver and gold; and as they carried or rolled the glittering dross ashore in their rags, with the perspiration falling from their brows like rain, we could not help exclaiming, ' Is it for this we trample on everything divine and human?'

KIRKDANDIE FAIR;
OR,
THE SMUGGLER'S REVENGE!

CHAPTER I.

WE never saw Kirkdandie Fair in its palmy days, but we had the happiness of seeing it ere its glory had entirely departed. We say *happiness*, for it was impossible for the most phlegmatic mortal to stand on the hill which commands it, and look down on the merry groups of lads and lasses assembled on the green beneath, without experiencing pleasureable sensations. In the foreground stood the solitary ruined chapel, about which history says little but that it was dedicated to the Holy Trinity, and emanated from the Church of Girvan, to which parish it formerly belonged. Strange as it may read, around that solitary old chapel, in the midst of a wild moorland district, from time immemorial was held a fair, which annually took place on the last Saturday of May. Being the only market in the year for the parishes of Girvan, Barr, Ballantrae, Colmonell, Straiton, and Dailly, it was numerously attended. Booths and stands were erected for the entertainment of the gathered throng and the disposal of merchandise, which, as there were no roads, was chiefly brought on horseback. Here those travelling merchants, whose avocation, like Othello's, is now gone, but who, before communication with the towns came to be so freely opened up, formed nearly the sole medium of sale or barter among the rural population, assembled in great numbers, bringing with them the tempting wares of England and the Continent. If, with the magician's power, we could recall a vision of Kirkdandie centuries ago, how grand and interesting would be the spectacle! The bivouac of the pedlars with their pack horses, who generally arrived the night before the fair; the bustle of active preparation by earliest dawn; and the gradual gathering

of the plaided and bonneted population, from the various path-
ways across the hills or down the straths, as the day advanced,
would be a picture of deep interest. Until recently, changed
as are the times, the gathering was a truly picturesque sight,
and one which, when once seen, could never be forgotten.

But besides the fame acquired by Kirkdandie as a market,
it was still more celebrated as the *Donnybrook* of Scotland.
The feuds of the year, whether new or old, were here reckoned
over, and generally settled by an appeal to physical force. It
was no uncommon thing, towards the close of the fair, to see
fifty or a hundred a-side engaged with fists or sticks, as chance
might favour. Smuggling, after the Union, became very pre-
valent throughout Scotland, and nowhere more so than in Ayrshire and Galloway. A great many small lairdships were then
in existence, the proprietors of which, almost to a man, were
associated for the purpose of carrying on a contraband trade.
From locality as well as union, they lived beyond the reach or
fear of the law. At Kirkdandie future operations were planned,
and old scores adjusted, though not always in an amicable
manner.

The fair day, on which our tale opens, was all that pleasure-
seekers could desire; and at an early hour lads and lasses
might have been seen in hundreds wending their way over the
hills to Kirkdandie.

Willie Brown, and Nannie, his sister, from the Ship Inn,
Girvan, had arrived the day before, bringing with them their
tent, and a youth about eighteen summers, who assisted them
to erect it in the most advantageous position. The landlord of
the Ship Inn was also captain and owner of the ' Maid of Carrick,' and famed far and near as a fearless smuggler. Nannie,
in common with the rest of the publicans towards the close of
the last century and beginning of this one, had always ' rowth
o' customers,' for, in addition to the goodness of the whisky,
she invariably brought in with the second half pint a large
supply of cakes, cheese, and haggis. Whether it was owing
to the ease with which Willie made his money, or the large-
ness and goodness of Nannie's heart, we cannot say, but the
Ship Inn was noted for a most liberal supply of eatables to
men on the spree. As the various groups began to arrive,
Brown stood at the door of his tent, in company with the youth
previously alluded to, describing the peculiarities of this and

that one, to the evident delight of his companion, whose dark eyes, although twinkling with merriment, seemed to read you at a glance.

'Here comes a lot o' my customers frae Girvan,' observed Brown. 'They're a' weavers, and real clever chiels some o' them are, although maistly Erish. That yin in front is a bit o' a poet like yersel', Robin.'

'Is he!' exclaimed the young man eagerly, 'I wish you could introduce me to him.'

'He'll likely be in here before the fair's over, but he's looked upon as a regular fule by his craft. Hearken hoo they're laughing at something he's been saying.'

'What's his name?' asked the young man.

'Billy Bannister.'

'What a curious name.'

'Oh, he's frae the north o' Ireland. Here's the beginning o' ane o' his sangs—for I hae him sometimes in wi' me—

'As I went down by Bloody Bridge,
Where there they sell strong beer and whisky o', etc.''

'Oh! curse ye, Brown!' exclaimed the young man, laughing immoderately, 'you're making that for my amusement.'

'I'm daein' naething o' the kind; Billy thinks it's first-class, and the weavers strengthen him in his opinion.'

'But is there not a celebrated bard belonging to the Barr?' inquired Robin. 'I think I've heard a poem of his in which he describes the Laird of Changue encountering the devil in a fair stand-up fight and vanquishing him.'

'Oh! the story goes that Changue sold himsel' to the deil for siller; but the truth is, Robin, M'Harg makes his money like mysel', by paying as little duty to the Government as possible. However, this has naething to do wi' the veracious laureate o' the hills. When the deil cam' to claim his bargain, Changue drew a circle wi' his sword, and, without invoking saint or scripture, invited his Satanic Majesty into the ring, and the battle began.

"The devil wi' his cloven foot
   Thought Changue out o'er the ring to kick,
But his sharp sword it made the slit
      A wee bit langer,
Auld clootie bit his nether lip
      Wi' spite an' anger.''

'The poet then goes on to describe how the deil got his sting, horns, and wings cut off, and then winds up in this manner—

> "Then clootie gaed a horrid hooh,
> And Changue, nae doot, was feared enough,
> But hit him hard across the mou'
>   Wi' his sharp steel;
> He tumbl't back oot ower the cleugh,
>   Changue nail'd the deil!"

'But as I'm an honest publican, here comes Changue.'

Scarcely had these words passed Brown's lips when the surly Laird o' Changue, accompanied by his winsome daughter Nannie, stepped forward and shook the publican's companion warmly by the hand, exclaiming, as he did so, 'Is it really possible, Burns, ye hae cam' a' the gate frae Kirk-oswald to see oor muirlan' lasses?'

'If the stock's anything like the sample ye hae brought along with you, Laird, I'll not regret my journey,' said Burns, as he bent his dark luminous eyes on the blushing maiden.

'If ye're pleased wi' the lassie, tak' her, in Gude's name, alang wi' ye, and let her see the fair, for I hae a little business to transact wi' the landlord o' the Ship.' Leaving the two celebrated smugglers to adjust their scores, and arrange their plans, Burns took the arm of the lovely girl, and, avoiding the throngest part of the fair, walked along in the direction of the ruined chapel, until they reached the holy well, in the rear of the hoary edifice. Inviting Nannie to sit down beside him, on a grassy mound, which commanded an admirable view of the fair, Burns, young as he then was, soon broke the barrier which existed between them as strangers, by the brilliancy of his wit, the keenness of his satire, and his inherent perception of the awkward and ridiculous in either man or woman. Burns, at this period of his life, was scarcely heard of beyond the circle in which he moved, and amongst the rustics with whom he associated he was known to be clever in conversation, and good at making a verse of a song, but that was all. In this manner they generally spoke of the heir of immortal fame. His social status was so low that he had to mix and mingle with men who, from want of education, could neither appreciate nor understand his genius.

As Nannie sat beside the man who was designed to sing her praises in deathless song, she felt fascinated by the easy flow of his conversation, and both the flight of time and her sweetheart were forgotten.

The noise and uproar of the fair was at its height. Pipers, fiddlers, and singers were surrounded by noisy groups of lads and lasses, dancing and yelling like bedlamites, when suddenly a fight commenced before the tent of Willie Brown, which in a moment threatened to put an end to the fair. Nannie sat until she saw her father engaged with the Laird of Chapeldonnan, and then rushed, with a scream, into the thickest of the *mèlee.*

CHAPTER II.

THE Ship Inn, occupied by Willie Brown and his sister Nannie, stands yet at the entrance of the old kirkyard of Girvan, but, like Kirkdandie, its glory and greatness has departed. At the present time, it resembles a man who has been on the " spree " for years, with threadbare coat and napless hat. In its present state of dilapidation, it would do credit to the worst rookery or slum in Britain. Indeed, it looks as if, at no distant date, it would tumble into the kirkyard it overlooks, and lie down quietly beside a number of its victims, who slumber peacefully in its shade.

The last time we saw the ' Old Ship,' as it is familiarly called by the residents, its windows were stuffed with straw and old hats, and it looked as if it had sent its last shred of respectability to it's *uncle's,* as many a good fellow did who frequented it. But, we would far rather record the virtues than the follies of our companions of earlier years.

> Some to Australia strayed afar ;
> Some tried their fortune on the main ;
> Some followed Colin Campbell's star ;
> Some found a grave on India's plain ;
> The wandering wind the requiem raves
> Of some who sleep beneath the waves.

But to resume: until recently, the ' Ship ' did a good business in spirits and with them, or there were many story-tellers in the parish.

Convenient to the ' Ship,' and in one of the low thatched

houses which formed the eastern boundary of the Kirkyard, resided Mrs Saunders, who had an only son named Jock. The old lady kept a twopenny lodging-house for the accommodation of both man and beast—the tramps generally bearing the latter animals on their backs.   Jock being, as has been already remarked, her only son, was apprenticed to the weaving, but, not liking the business, he took to drinking whisky, at which he earned a considerable amount of celebrity.   In consequence of Jock's predilection for alcohol, he was seldom absent from the 'Ship,' and, as a tumbler full was neither here nor there to the jolly captain of the 'Maid of Carrick,' Jock became a sort of appendage to the Inn, and as such, learned and knew many of its secrets.

Jock was admired generally by the patrons of the 'Ship' for his goodness of temper, obliging manners, and strange eccentricities.   Under the influence of drink, he had one song that he invariably sung and acted, called ' The Crow.' In the execution of this strange composition he generally stood on a chair, and when it came to the part where the ' Crow ' was supposed to fly, he effected this difficult feat by flapping with his long bony arms, and falling from whatever pedestal he was perched on upon the floor, from which he had generally to be carried to his mother's *padding kane.*

Now to every customer who frequented the ' Ship,' except the Laird of Chapeldounan, Jock would perform for a glass. He had taken an aversion to the Laird, and neither threats nor whisky would induce him to sing to M'Crindle. For this obstinacy the Laird hated him, and Jock sincerely reciprocated the feeling.

' Are ye gaun to sing me the "Crow " to-day ?' shouted the Laird, as Jock entered Brown's tent at Kirkdandie.

' No, I'm blest if I do,' answered Jock, who spoke with a hard Irish accent.

' Then I'll make ye, ye ugly looking scarecrow,' cried the Laird, griping the half-starved wretch by the neck, and nearly shaking him out of his old black coat.

' Come, come, Chapeldounan, hands off,' cried Changue.

' Mind yer ain affairs, M'Harg ; I'll make him perform to me, or I'll pitch him into the Stinchar.'

' That was the way you served Glentig from Ballantrae, ye murdering scoundrel, because he wouldn't let you have his 'brandy for nothing,' shouted Jock, who had now safely retreated behind Changue.

This allusion to Glentig was an unpardonable offence, because it was true, and brandishing his heavy cudgel he aimed a savage blow at Jock, which missing him, fell with a thud on the right shoulder of Changue.

'I had it in for ye at ony rate, ye false loon,' cried Changue, as he brought his oaken staff, with fearful effect, over the head of the Laird of Chapeldonnan.

In a moment all was confusion and uproar, and, as each had their partizans in the fair, the fight soon became general.

Burns, who had rushed after Nannie, soon found himself in the midst of the drunken mob, but like many others in the world, he found it easier getting into troubled waters than escaping out of them. Hither and thither he was borne along with the infuriated mob. Tents were overthrown, stands of valuable goods trampled on; and men fell fast, amidst the cries of 'Girvan for ever!' 'Weel done, Ballantrae!' 'Haud to the loons, Changue, for the credit o' the Barr!' and similar war cries. How the fight would have terminated is hard to conjecture, had not the cry of 'The Coastguard is coming!' been heard above the din of battle.

In a moment hostilities ceased, and all ranged themselves under the dauntless Laird of Changue. No matter what the feud might be, the Revenue Officers were regarded as the common enemy of all, and as such they unitedly prepared to resist them.

'I'll tell ye what it is, freens,' cried Changue, as he took off his Kilmarnock bonnet and wiped the perspiration from his brow, 'it's weel enough kent that they're here after Jamie Gordon, the mate o' the "Maid o' Carrick," wha's noo alang wi' the skipper in the tent ower there, an' if ye allow him to be captured by the landsharks wha hae made a descent on the fair, never say ye belang to the land o' Bruce again.'

A vociferous cheer greeted this harangue, and every man flourished his stick in defiance of the coastguardsmen, who, numbering about a dozen, stood at a short distance with drawn cutlasses, and pistols in their belts.

'Let us rally round Captain Brown's tent,' again shouted Changue, 'and let the lubbers dare to touch him.'

But Changue's advice came too late, for Captain Thomson,

F

who commanded the coastguards, had been secretly informed, by a paid spy, that Gordon was in Brown's tent, and had, like an experienced officer, divided his men into two divisions, leaving one party among the brushwood which grew along the banks of the Stinchar, with strict orders not to move until the annual fight took place when the tents would be sure to be emptied, and then to capture Gordon, while he and his division lay down on the hillside that overlooked the fair.

As Changue and his followers were preparing to defend Brown's tent a shrill whistle was heard from the hill above them, and to the great astonishment of the smugglers they beheld Thomson withdraw his men and leave them in undisturbed possession of the ground.

' Curse ye for a set of cowardly loons,' cried Nannie Brown, rushing frantically in among Changue's bodyguard. ' Is it no a nice thing to see ane o' the best smugglers on the Carrick coast borne awa' a prisoner, while the men o' Kirkoswald, Girvan, and Ballantrae are staunin' staring at ane anither like silly nowts ? '

' Miss Brown, ye're clean demented. What dae ye mean ? ' demanded Changue.

' What dae I mean ? ' reiterated Nannie, scornfully ; ' dae ye see Thomson and his men gaun ower the hill yonder ? Weel, he has got Jamie Gordon along with him a prisoner ! '

A yell of rage and disappointment greeted this announcement. To complete the dismay of the smugglers, Nannie burst into tears.

' It canna be helped,' said Changue, in a desponding tone, ' for before we could reach the tap o' the hill, the coastguardsmen wad be nearly at the " Seven Sisters." But, cheer up, Miss Brown ! I hae helped a frien' oot o' a waur scrape than this.'

With this assurance, Nannie was obliged to be satisfied, and retired, wringing her hands and sobbing bitterly, to the tent, followed by all the leading smugglers of the district.

While these stirring incidents were transpiring, Burns remained passively looking on. The fame of the fair had induced him to visit it, but if the deeper emotions of his highly sensitive nature were stirred, it was with contempt and abhorrence. Beauty, wit, and sentiment had for him irresistible charms ; but anything savouring, in the least degree, of savage brutality made him shudder. Seeing, therefore, that the storm had subsided, he approached Nannie with the intention of bidding her good-bye.

'Ye micht come hame wi' me,' said Nannie, with her sweetest smile, 'for it's mair than probable my faither will gang to Girvan to-night and see what cau be done to extricate Gordon oot o' his difficulties.'

Burns' heart was made of too tender material to resist such an invitation, so, after bidding Brown and his sister good evening, he started for the Changue.

CHAPTER III.

'STUMPY,' the ancient prison of Girvan, stood on the spot now occupied by the Town's Buildings. It was anything but a pretentious, awe-inspiring edifice, but it was equal to the requirements of the age; for, notwithstanding our boasted civilization, crime has increased. Then, Jamie Ross, an old, respectable man, who acted in the double capacity of bellman and officer, was quite sufficient to keep the town and country around it in order; now it requires three or four policemen to discharge the onerous duties of the parish. The population was nearly as great, and men drank as much, if not more than they do now; but as a celebrated toper, named M. Govannie, once remarked to us—*The whisky was better.*

But to return to our tale. The fair of Kirkdandie was ended, but not the spirit of animosity and revenge engendered at it. Jamie Gordon, the mate of the 'Maid of Carrick,' was safely consigned to 'Stumpy;' and in the parlour of the Ship Inn were assembled Willie Brown, the landlord; Jamie M'Harg, of Changue; Adams, of Glentig, and Nannie, the hostess and the affianced bride of Gordon.

'Something maun be dune the nicht, lads,' observed Brown, meditatively, 'for ye see he will be hoisted off to Ayr in the morning.'

'That's what I hae been thinking about since we left the fair, an' I'll be hanged if I can see my road at a',' said Changue.

'Nannie here micht help us a wee, but I'm amaist ashamed to suggest what I was thinking about,' said Glentig.

' If it's onything that I can dae to assist puir Jamie, ye may depend on me doing my best, Laird,' cried Nannie, eagerly.

' It's weel eneuch kent he's yer lad,' observed Glentig, ' through the hale toon.'

' I suppose sae,' answered Nannie, demurely; 'but I dinna see hoo that's to help him, puir fallow !'

' But I dae. Ross will allow ye in to see him, when he wouldna thraw the key in the lock for me.'

' Oh ! I daresay I could get in to see him in the morning.'

' But ye maun see him to-night. It's scarcely ten o'clock. Tak' ower a bottle o' brandy wi' ye, and gie it to Ross. Tell him ye want to speak twa or three words to Jamie, and be sure to be greetin' at the time.'

' She'll manage that pairt o' the business nicely,' interrupted her brother, drily.

' Silence, Willie, tae we hear the plot,' interposed Changue.

' He'll hardly refuse ye admittance, and as sune as ever ye win in, cast aff yer cap and gown, mak' Jamie don them as quickly as he can, and march oot. Of course, ye'll hae to remain in " Stumpy " till the morning.'

' Bravo ! Glentig,' shouted Changue.

' That's a capital scheme.'

' Dinna halloo till ye're oot o' the wud,' said the landlord o' the ' Ship,' quietly. ' The plan's guid enough, but it's the winning in is the great difficulty.'

' But it's worth a trial at ony rate,' persisted Glentig.

As it was the only feasible plan the smugglers could think of, and as Nannie was impatient to be gone, they agreed to make the trial.

Suggesting to Nannie the propriety of putting on two gowns, so as she would have one to spare for her sweetheart, in the course of a few minutes she was tripping across the ' Flushes ' to the residence of the town officer, and as he lived convenient to ' Stumpy,' she reached it by eleven o'clock.

As soon as Nannie knocked at the door, Mr Ross demanded who wanted to see him at such an untimely hour of the night.

' A frien frae the " Ship." Open the door, Mr Ross, I'll no' detain ye a minute.'

' Oh ! it's you, Nannie,' said the town's officer, as he unbarred the door. ' I was preparing to gang to bed; but come awa' ben a minute.'

'There's a drap o' brandy Willie sent ower, an' ye may swear it's guid,' said Nannie, reaching him the bottle.

'The proof o' the puddin's the preeing o't,' observed Mr Ross, as he lifted a tumbler off the dresser and poured out a lucky glass, tasted it, smacked his lips approvingly, and then remarked mentally, 'It's no for naething the glede whistles,' but he added aloud, 'it's real guid.'

'I'm glad it pleases ye, for I am gaun to ask a great favour frae ye.'

'I was thinkin' sae, Miss Brown,' said the town official, with as stern a look as he could assume; for he felt confident Nannie's visit had reference to his prisoner.

'I wad be for ever yer debtor, Mr Ross, if ye wad let me in to see Jamie for a minute or sae.'

'It's as muckle as my coat's worth, Nannie, to do anything o' the kind,' interrupted Mr Ross. 'I'm bound to produce him in the morning; and ye ken Thomson has been maist anxious to secure him this mony a day.'

'I ken a' that,' replied Nannie, bursting into tears. 'But if he's marched off to Ayr in the morning, I may never see him again. Oh! what am I to dae?'

'Confound Thomson and the coastguard baith!' exclaimed Ross, who might have resisted the soothing effects of the brandy, but not the handsome maiden's tears; 'I'll let ye in to see him for ten minutes. I suppose the street's quiet?'

'I never met a livin' body frae I left the "Ship" till I came here.'

'Weel, ye wadna meet mony deid anes, I'm thinking; but as they're yer door neighbours ye should ken mair aboot them than me,' said Ross, laughing, as he lifted the lantern and led the way to 'Stumpy.'

Looking cautiously around him, he whispered to Nannie not to wait over ten minutes, and then opened the door and admitted her, taking the precaution, however, of locking it after her.

Nannie had been scarcely five minutes inside, when a low rap announced the interview to be over, and Nannie, as he supposed, emerged with her head muffled in her plaid—a custom yet common in the district.

'Ye haena been lang,' observed the good-hearted jailer, as he carefully locked the door. 'Puir thing, she's cryin' that sair that she canna speak,' he muttered, as he watched her walking rapidly away in the direction of the Ship Inn.

The room in which the smugglers sat, during Nannie's absence, had a door which opened into the kirkyard, and they knew if Gordon effected his escape, it would be through it he would come in.

Strange as it may appear to some of our young readers, the door which communicated with the churchyard, like every other back-door attached to public-houses, was the best paying entrance. When it is borne in mind that until recently the ' Holy Fair,' or ' Preachings,' in connection with the dispensation of the Sacrament, was held here yearly, and that everyone was supposed to take a refreshment between the services, it can easily be imagined the necessity there was for a door opening into the kirkyard. Those who have never witnessed a scene of the kind may consider Burns' ' Holy Fair ' a piece of exaggerated profanity, but it is literally true. On Preaching Saturday morning, old and young might have been seen hurrying to the churchyard, carrying deals, chairs, and stools, and securing the most advantageous positions for hearing the ministers from the various parishes around. There was no Free Kirk then, and but few dissenters of any denomination, consequently, when the population of four or five parishes congregated together, all more or less dry, the Ship Inn did a roaring trade.

But if the door, opening into the graveyard, afforded the ' godly thrang ' the easy means of ingress and egress to the ' Ship,' its facilities for smugglers were invaluable. The only barrier between the shore and the ' Ship ' was the low wall which ran along the west side of the kirkyard. Of course the Girvan water was to cross, but this was but a trifling affair to a class who might be considered amphibious.

' There's some one rapping at the back door,' exclaimed the Laird of Changue, interrupting Glentig in the midst of a most exciting affray with the coastguard at Ballantrae.

' Nannie has scarcely time to be back yet,' observed the landlord, rising and going towards the door. Unbarring the door, he peeped cautiously out, and, to his evident chagrin, he perceived no one but Jock Saunders.

' Could ye no hae come in by the front door, ye hungry looking thief!' exclaimed Brown, in a tone that was anything but complimentary.

'No,' answered Jock, mysteriously, 'I was afraid of being seen by Chapeldonnan, who is hovering about, in company with the captain of the coastguard. Let me in, I have something to tell you that will astonish you and your friends.'

Jock Saunders, although fond of a dram, was as great a coward as ever trod the earth, and the fearless landlord of the 'Ship' knew this well. Gripping Jock, therefore, unceremoniously by the collar of his old black coat, he dragged him inside and shut the door.

'Whaur hae ye been since ye left the fair?' asked the landlord, as soon as he had given him a glass to put the 'shaking' off him.

'At the back window of the Star Inn, listening to a conversation between Chapeldonnan and Capt. Thomson aboot you,' answered Jock.

'Tak' care noo, Jock, what ye're saying, for ye ken ye sometimes shoot wi' a lang bow.'

'That I may never drink another glass—'

'Whist! we want nae swearin' here. Tell us, like a decent chiel, what ye heard?'

'Well, you know whether you and Chapeldonnan have made a bargain about a cargo of whisky or not.'

'Weel. What mair?' asked the landlord.

'To be delivered to him at the Howe Port, by you or Glentig.'

'What mair did ye hear at the back window, man? Oot wi't at ance. Ye ken ye're amang friens here,' exclaimed the landlord, while an ominous frown rested on his weather-beaten face.

'He's to let Thomson know to an hour when you will be there, and of course he will be waiting to secure you and the crew of the "Maid of Carrick."'

'Was there naething said aboot siller, Jock? Glentig, help him to anither dram,' said the landlord, who kept pacing the room like a caged tiger.

'Whatever money Chapeldonnan pays you for the cargo, Thomson has promised to repay him double for the information, and, to throw you off your guard, he's to call to-morrow and apologise for the row in the fair to-day.'

'There's a croon to ye, Jock. Noo, rin awa' hame like a decent lad, an' I'll gie ye and Charlie Johnstone yer mornin' when ye call.'

'God bless you, Captain,' exclaimed Jock, as he surveyed the five shilling piece with delight.

'Nae blarney, Jock, rin awa'.'

'I would like the smallest sensation in a bottle to keep me company through the night, if your honour would kindly give it to me,' said Jock, offering back the money.

'There's a bottle, noo be off an' see Sal the cobbler as quick as ye like.'

'May I never drink another glass—'

A rap at the back door cut short his protestation, and Brown, who was in no amiable temper, dragged him to the front door, shoved him out and bolted it, and then hurried to the back and admitted Jamie Gordon.

After laughing heartily at the row there would be about 'Stumpy' in the morning, when Thomson would come to convey his prisoner to Ayr, they commenced to discuss the best mode of revenging the base conduct of Chapeldonnan. To the smugglers of Carrick his character was well known. That he was greedy, mean, and grasping to the last degree, they were perfectly aware, but none of them thought he would so basely betray the men with whom he associated. There could be no doubt now but Gordon's capture was attributable to him, and when they were calm enough to compare notes, many and bitter were the imprecations invoked on his head. After a long and stormy debate, it was finally agreed to adopt Brown's plan of revenge; but we must not anticipate its denouement.

CHAPTER IV.

HAVING settled the above point to their entire satisfaction, Gordon's affairs next occupied their attention.

'Ye must leave this immediately, Jamie,' observed Brown, 'for ye'll no be safe here in the morning.'

'Is the "Maid" lying at the wharf?' asked Glentig.

Brown nodded his head affirmatively.

'Then the best thing Jamie can dae is to tak' the boat up to the Ardwell Bay, and hing aboot there till we see Nannie out in the morning. Wi' this licht easterly win' he can hug the lan' as close as he likes. Munro will gang alang wi' him.'

Leaving the party to enjoy themselves as they could, the

landlord of the 'Ship' started for the Braehead, to rouse Willie Munro. By the time he returned, day was beginning to break, and the whole party started at once for the Wooden Wharf, where the 'Maid of Carrick' was lying. Not a house then stood on the spot now known as Newton Kennedy, neither was the Water of Girvan spanned by the wooden bridge which has excited the admiration of every stranger who ever beheld it—not for its architectural beauty; it makes no pretensions either to originality of design or elaborate workmanship, but as a monument of the liberality of a great *Liberal* to his poor feuars, it is unsurpassed in Scotland.

Brown and his party, having reached the Wharf in safety, waited till they saw the 'Maid of Carrick' safely over the bar, and then returned to the 'Ship' to snatch an hour's sleep. Throughout the whole town it was well known that Jamie Gordon, the smuggler, was in 'Stumpy;' and at an early hour, although it was Sunday, a great number had assembled at the Cross, waiting for the opening of the public-houses—for in those days Forbes Mackenzie was unknown—as well as the arrival of the coastguard, who, with the bulk of the inhabitants, stood as high in their estimation as a policeman is supposed to do now in the eyes of the inmates of a bridewell.

So anxious was Chapeldonnan to see Gordon brought forth, that he had remained at the 'Star Inn' all night; but not wishing to appear in any connection with the coastguardsmen, he had warned the Captain not to recognize him if he saw him among the crowd of onlookers.

'There's Thomson awa into Ross's,' observed Jamie Enterkine, from Leggenwhully. 'They'll shune be bringing him out noo.'

'And much credit they'll get by the same honourable job,' replied Billy Houston, a weaver from the north of Ireland, whose father rented a good farm at home; but Billy was a wild boy, and ran over to Scotland, bringing with him a wealthy farmer's daughter, that he invariably called by the euphonious name of 'Jinny.' Poor Jinny had left home in such haste that she neglected to put on a gown, consequently she lived and died in a shortgown and petticoat, the latter article scarcely covering her knees.

'Yonder comes Chapeldonnan roun' the Auld Kirk,' cried John M'Quaker.

'And by the powers o' Moll Kelly,' exclaimed Billy Houston, 'here comes Changue and Glentig over the Flushes. Boys, do ye think there's going to be a rescue?'

Rab M'Harg, the hosier, said, 'I dinna think it; the law is ower strong tae attempt ouything o' the kind.'

Billy Houston exclaimed that he didn't think anything of the kind; but at this moment Mr Ross appeared in knee breeches and blue coat, trimmed with red, carrying in his right hand a massive key, and followed by four men wearing the Government livery, so in a second a death-like stillness pervaded the noisy group. 'Make room, boys, for the town officer,' shouted Billy Houston, as loud as he could roar, when he saw Mr Ross close upon him.

'Shut yer mouth, or I'll put my thumb in yer throat, ye starved abortion,' hissed a gruff voice in his ear, and on turning round Billy found himself iu close proximity to the powerful Laird of Changue.

An ominous silence pervaded the group of hardy fishermen assembled at 'Stumpy' corner, during the brief time the myrmidons of the law were inside the prison; but when Ross and the Captain of the Coastguard emerged, leading between them the bonnie buxom hostess of the 'Ship,' in place of the fearless smuggler, Jamie Gordon, a derisive cheer burst from the assembled inhabitants, so loud and prolonged that it completely drowned the angry altercation between Ross and Thomson.

Chapeldonnan found his limbs shaking beneath his weight, but smothering his indignation, he advanced to Captain Brown, and holding out his hand, said—'I hope there's nae ill will between us on account o' the bit tulzie yesterday?'

'Nane in the world, Chapeldonnan,' replied Brown, suppressing his inclination to throttle him where he stood. 'Come awa' ower to the "Ship," and get a bite o' breakfast.' As Brown said this, he took the arm of his sister, and walked away to the 'Ship Inn,' followed by Chapeldonnan, Changue, and Glentig.

Men who are bad, and make no pretence of being good, are pitied, but men who pretend to be good, and are really bad, are despised. Chapeldonnan belonged to the latter class. In company with such men as Brown, his schemes for defrauding the revenue were many, but in the presence of a revenue officer he affirmed that he was only discharging his moral obligations to society by informing on smugglers. He was all things to all men, not for the purpose of doing them good, but to work their ruin if it filled his coffers. A moneyless man was quite safe in his company, but he made it a rule to associate as little as possible with such a class. An astute Government officer like Captain Thomson could estimate his character nicely, and if his life and property had been in danger he would have entrusted it more readily to the keeping of the most notorious smuggler rather than to him.

As Chapeldonnan followed Brown and his mate over the 'Flushes' to the 'Ship,' he mentally thought that they never suspected him of treachery, else he would not have been invited to breakfast; but if he had known what was passing through the mind of some of the men walking by his side, he would have hesitated to enter the house which overlooked the grave-yard. Leaving the smugglers at their breakfast, let us return for a moment to 'Stumpy' corner.

It is impossible to describe the rage and mortification of Thomson and his men as they departed, followed by the jeers and laughter of the fishermen. Thomson, as he entered Mr Ross's house, consoled himself with the thought that before the end of the week he would have the whole gang in custody.

'This is a bad job, Ross, I doubt, for you,' observed the revenue officer as he seated himself on a chair, and gazed moodily at the fire.

'It's an awkward affair, and I'm sorry for't,' said the jailer, quietly.

'Awkward affair,' echoed the Captain, angrily. 'I tell ye to your face, Ross, it's a piece of cursed jobbery. How much did you get for letting Gordon out?'

'Honestly, I know nothing about it; but I hae an observation to mak that'll be perhaps displeasing to a man o' your position and integrity—Ill doers are aye ill dreaders.'

'Villain! what do you mean by this?' exclaimed the Captain, starting to his feet and confronting the jailer.

'Simply that yer loof has been greased before noo, else ye wadna be sae ready to suspect ithers. Sit doon, Mr Thomson, an' keep a calm sough, for I ken mair things than you think.'

'Ye low infernal scamp!' cried Thomson, furiously, 'I'll strip that coat off your back before the end of the week.'

As he said this he stepped towards the door.

'Stop a minute, tae I whisper a word in yer lug that I never wad hae uttered but for your cursed bullying impudence. Glentig wadna be sitting noo in the "Ship" had ye no been weel paid for't. Noo ye can gang hame and tak' yer breakfast aff that—there's the door.'

'Mr Ross, my dear sir, speak lower. I had no intention, upon my honour, of doing you the least harm.'

'Weel, weel, we'll let byeganes be byeganes,' said Ross, wiping the perspiration from his brow; 'here's a drop o' brandy that I doot hisna paid the Government dues, but it's real guid for a' that.'

'This cursed business is never to be mentioned again,' said Thomson, taking the glass, and drinking it off.

'Never by me,' replied Ross.

'I'm satisfied; good morning.'

'That's the way to satisfy folk,' muttered Ross, as he went to the door, and looked after him until he turned up Tarry Lane.

During breakfast, in the 'Ship,' a stranger would never have suspected anything wrong between the four gentlemen seated at the table. Not a frown was discernible on one of their faces. Glentig told his rattling stories without the least restraint, but he took the precaution, nevertheless, to tell only tales which might be repeated with safety at the Cross. Brown and Changue were in the best possible spirits, and, as for Nannie, her face was radiant with joy. Her dear Jamie was again out of the clutches of the law, and the thought that he was free constituted her happiness. All these things combined to lull the suspicious nature of Chapeldonnan into a false security. Like every villain he was a consummate hypocrite, and he sat and rubbed his hands with apparent delight, exclaiming, as he did so, that it was the best managed piece of work ever he saw, and that Nannie was worth a mine of gold to a fearless, clever fellow like Gordon.

'Did ye hear that compliment, Nance?' asked Glentig, laughing.

'Ou, ay, I'm listening,' answered Nannie, dryly.

'I hope, friens, ye hae nae ill-will aboot the squabble yesterday?' inquired Chapeldonnau.

'Never mention it, Laird, again. Ye ken when drink's in wit's oot,' observed Brown.

'Then I suppose ye intend to adhere to yer bargain aboot the liquor?'

' Certainly ! Did ye think onything else ?' inquired Brown, with a look of surprise.

' Oh! I didna ken but ye micht hae changed yer mind, seeing we hae been sae unfortunate of late. But since ye're gaun to rin the risk, ye'll better make it twa hunner and fifty pounds worth, instead o' what we were speaking aboot. Ye see, friens, I like to encourage trade,' said Chapeldonnan, looking round complacently on the smugglers.

' Mony thanks for yer patronage,' said Brown ; ' but seeing yer order is sae large, recollect whenever the boat touches the shore, I'll be looking for the cash, so ye see ye maun be prepared to run a little risk as weel as the lave.'

' As sune as ye rin into the Howe Port, I'll pay doon the cash. Noo, friens, if bowls row richt, I may expect ye on Friday nicht ?'

' Wind and weather permitting,' said Glentig, with a laugh.

' Weel, I maun bid ye guid morning, for, as I'm in the toon onyway, I wadna like to miss the kirk.' Starting to his feet, he shook them all warmly by the hand, and wished them a safe run.

' Weel, of a' the cursed villains ever crossed my bows, that's the greatest,' observed Changue, staring after him. ' Brown, if ye had taken my advice, he wad hae lift the back door o' the " Ship " in a sheet the nicht aboot twal o'clock.'

' I wadna ware a sheet on him,' observed Glentig.

' And be hung for a carrion like him. Na, my lads ! My plan's a safe ane, and he will remember my revenge while he lives, for I believe he's fonder o' siller than life ; but, whist! here comes Nannie, and we'll sune hae to be jogging up the shore,' said Brown.

' Bless me, Nannie, whaur are ye gaun ? I hope ye're no for the kirk along wi' Chapeldonnan,' exclaimed Glentig, as he surveyed Nannie, arrayed in her best silk gown.

' I'm gaun alang wi' ye to see Jamie.'

' And wha'll mind the house ?' inquired her brother.

' The house can mind itsel' for an hour or twa ; there's naething a daein' at onyrate.'

' Weel, I maun awa hame, friens,' said Changue, rising ; ' but depend upon me being at the Howe Port on Friday nicht, and if I can induce Rabbie Burns to bide till then I'll bring him down wi' me to see the sport. Gude-bye, and success, my hearties.'

CHAPTER V.

WHILE the smugglers were discussing their plans of profit and revenge in the Ship Inn, Burns sat on a green hillside in the vicinity of the Changue, in company with the heroine of one of his best love songs. It was the first day of rosy June and of the week. Nothing broke the solemn stillness which pervaded valley and mountain save the cry of the plover and the bleating of sheep. Around them were springing a thousand beauteous flowers in all the glorious freshness of early summer, while the low humming of the bees, as they flitted from flower to flower, mingled with the running of a tiny burn at their side, carried the enthusiastic youthful bard unconsciously into the regions of dreamland. Everything around him touched a chord which vibrated to the innermost recesses of his heart. The mighty hills seemed to spurn the earth and ascend to the ethereal regions of light and love, while the sunbeams as they danced and glistened on the pellucid waters of the Stinchar, appeared like the silvery fragments of a shattered world. So different, so grand, so great, was the scenery of this wild moorland district to that which surrounded bleak Lochlea, a farm rented by his sire in the parish of Tarbolton, that he heaved a deep sigh of ecstatic delight. Nor is this to be wondered at, when it is borne in mind that he was only eighteen years of age, and had only been permitted to go to Kirkoswald during the summer months to learn mensuration, until autumn would summon him to resume the sickle.

'What are ye sighing aboot, Robin? I haena the least doot, for a' yer fine speeches to me, but ye're thinking lang aboot some o' the Kirkoswald lasses,' said Nannie, looking archly in his face.

Nannie unconsciously had hit the mark, for at that moment a vision of the peerless Peggy Thomson flitted before him, and mentally he was wishing she was present to share his joy.

'There's bonnie lasses aboot Kirkoswald, Nannie, but believe me, they couldna compete with the maidens of the Barr if beauty was the prize they were contending for,' answered Burns, gallantly.

'When ye think sae much o' them,' said Nannie, blushing, 'ye micht be coaxed to immortalize some o' them in verse.'

'It's maybe not to do, and I can tell ye her name—but I daresay ye'll be nae way curious,' said Burns, smiling, as he bent upon her blushing face his dark, lovelit eyes.

'What a man! Did anybody ever hear the like o' that? I'm nae hypocrite, Robin, au I'm deein' wi' curiosity to hear her name.'

'Could ye no' guess?'

'No.'

Burns put his arms around her waist and whispered in her ear—'Nannie. Noo, I think that deserves a kiss.'

'Let me hear a verse, an' I'll tell ye whether or no.'

> 'Her face is fair, her heart is true,
> She's spotless as she's bonny, O;
> The opening gowan wet wi' dew,
> Nae purer is than Nannie, O.'

As Burns repeated this verse, and gazed admiringly on her fair face, the young Laird of Munoncion was in danger of losing his sweetheart.

'If the rest o' the sang's like that, it's worth a' ye bargained for, an' mair,' observed Nannie, laughing.

'If I begin, I may, like Adam in Paradise, gang on till I ruin a'.'

'Halloo! Robin, lad, ye're makin' unca free wi' ither folk's property,' cried the Laird of Changue, as he cantered up to where Burns and his daughter were sitting. 'But I commend Nannie's taste—hae ye seen her lad?'

'For gudesake, faither, haud yer tongue,' said Nannie, blushing like a peony.

'He's no' an ill-looking fallow, Munoncion,' continued her father, aggravatingly, 'was it no' for his feet an' hands; the former's like coal scuttles, and the latter's no' unlike frying pans—but he's rich, Robin, as a Jew.'

Nannie did not linger to hear her lad described by her father, but hurried away, with tears standing in her eyes and a wish in her heart that Munoncion was at the Antipodes.

'Money covers a multitude o' faults,' observed Burns, sighing.

'An' sins tae, Robin. But if ye hae a fancy for the lassie, ye'll get her, an' welcome for me—but I'm havering—come awa' hame an' get some dinner.'

Leading the pony by the bridle, the laird walked leisurely

along towards the Changue. On the way thither, he briefly
informed Burns of the premeditated treachery of Chapeldonnau,
and of the low, mean part he had acted in the capture of
Gordon.

'He must be an unprincipled scamp,' exclaimed Burns,
warmly, 'to worm himself into the confidence of any party
merely for the sake of betraying them.'

'It's no a'thegither for that, but he's heart greedy. The
coifs aboot the Barr hae a story afloat aboot me sellin' mysel'
to the deil for siller, but if I had been that fond o't, I micht hae
been as rich as Munoncion.'

'But how do you intend to act respecting Chapeldonnan?'
inquired Burns.

'I ken hoo I wad hae acted, but the skipper of the "Maid o'
Carrick" 's a queer chiel, an' canna think o' resortin' tae cruelty
at a'.'

'Perhaps Brown's right. The best method with such characters is to have naething to do wi' them,' observed Burns.

'Maybe, Robin; but the Laird o' Chapeldonnan's no' gaun
to get oot o' oor clutches sae easy as that.'

As they were now in sight of the Changue, the laird began
and briefly narrated Brown's plan of revenge, which he had
scarcely finished when Burns burst into an immoderate fit of
laughing, declaring at the same time it was the best ever he
had heard. 'Brown's quite right,' he cried; 'to a man such
as Chapeldonnan it will be a fearful punishment.'

'When the scheme pleases ye sae weel, Robin, ye should
wait to Friday nicht an' see it carried oot.'

'l canna weel do that; but I'll tell ye what I'll do; I'll
tell Graham and Thomson, an' we'll rin doon to the Howe Port
frae the Maidenheads on Friday evening to see the sport.'

'I wad rather ye wad wait, and I'm sure sae wad Nannie.
Indeed I promised to Brown to bring ye doon wi' me on Friday
nicht.'

Burns would willingly have remained at the Changue, but
he had an appointment with Peggy Thomson on Monday night,
which at this passionate period of his life he would not have
broken for the reputed wealth of Munoncion. Nor was his
love for Peggy evanescent. For some years he steadily entertained the idea of wedding her; therefore all Changue's friendly
importunity could not induce him to stay longer than the

following morning. Firmly as Burns had refused Changue to sojourn at his house until Friday, he found his resolution evaporating when subjected to the witching glances of Nannie; and, on the next day, when she accompanied him a part of the way over the hills to Kirkoswald, had she renewed her solicitations, she would have stormed his vulnerable heart. Like all true poets he was deeply susceptible of the beautiful, and when he held out his hand to the artless, lovely girl who had inspired his muse, and gazed into her deep blue eyes, suffused with tears, Peggy Thomson was for a moment forgotten; but no sooner had Nannie's fair form disappeared among the hills than his heart returned to its allegiance to Peggy, and as he journeyed along, he busied himself composing the beautiful song beginning—

> ' Now westlin winds and slaught'ring guns
> Bring Autumn's pleasant weather.'

CHAPTER VI.

ALTHOUGH Jamie Gordon had effected his escape he felt anything but happy. The thought that he would have to remain in Arran, perhaps, for a considerable time, was very unpleasant; notwithstanding the hearty welcome he anticipated from Duncan Currie. Had Miss Brown been residing in Glencloy it would have reconciled him to his exile for any length of time; but with thirty miles of sea rolling betwixt him and her, the thought was intolerable.

With the light puff of easterly wind, which prevailed in the morning, he kept cruizing closely along the shore, from Ardwell Bay to Ardmillan Point, until noon. During the whole of this time the glass was scarcely five minutes from his eye; not that he was afraid of Brown and Glentig keeping their appointment, but he was doubtful if Nannie would shut up the ' Ship' and accompany them. Every inch of the road from Shalloch to Ardwell was scanned a hundred times over, before he observed them coming briskly along the road. ' Yonder they're coming at last, Munro!' he exclaimed joyfully, ' an' I'm blest if Nannie's no alang wi' them.'

' I'm glad to hear 't, Jamie, for it's my opinion if they hadna hove in sicht sune ye were in the fair way o' gaun mad.'

G

'Thiuk on what she has done for me, Willie,' pleaded Gordon in extenuation of his anxiety. 'If it hadna been for her I wadna be cruizing here, I'm thinking.'

'She's a noble lass, nae doot, but——'

'Nae buts aboot it,' cried Gordon, impatiently; 'I tell thee, Munro, she's worth gold.'

'I had the same opinion o' Sally before we got spliced; but I can assure ye, mate, that she seemed anything but an angel lying in bed this morning, wi' her snuffy nose, and a cap on her heid that appeared to be washed in the tatie pcuriu's au' bleached up the lum.'

'Starboard your helm a wee, Willie; steady at that—she's tripping alang nicely noo. I wad like to see the cutter could overhaul the "Maid" in calm or storm.'

'She's a fine boat, but I think we're near enough the land.'

'I daresay we are,' said Gordon, as he ran forward and hauled in the jib and foresail.

They were now within hailing distance of the party on the shore, so, jumping into the "punt," Gordon bent to the oars, and in a few minutes he was standing beside Nannie on the thyme-wreathed rocks.

'We'll awa' on board, Glentig,' observed Brown aside, 'an' allow them half an hour for palaver.'

Without a word of warning they both sprang into the boat and shoved off, and left the lovers standing together.

'When ye're weary o' the rocks, Jamie, ye can hoist a flag o' distress, and we'll tak' ye on board,' cried Glentig, laughing.

The rapture of Haidee and Don Juan was not more ecstatic, when they wandered hand in hand along the shore of their island home, than that experienced by Nannie and Jamie, 'for to their young eyes each seemed an angel, and earth paradise.'

What a blessed period of life is youth! We may be surrounded by dangers and difficulties that appal the man of age and experience; but, far away beyond the ominous cloud of adversity youth descries the effulgent star of Hope, and rushes onward like the boy 'bearing the banner with the strange device—Excelsior.' So it was with Gordon and Miss Brown. Seated on the rocks covered with sea-pinks and thyme, the machinations and plots of Chapledonnan seemed like the airy web of the gossamer. Away in the future they saw—not a large account at the bank—but a cosie cottage, a trig boat, and rosy children, blest with health and plenty to eat; and the vision was so enchanting that the tears stood in Nannie's eyes contemplating it. How long they would have sat in this entranced state we have no means of determining, but the hoarse matter of fact voice of Glentig summoned them from dreams to realities.

'Hallo, Jamie, lad, it's time we were shaping for Arran. This licht easterly wnn will tak' us there in a jiffey.'

'Ay, ay, sir. I'll be there in a minute.' As he said this he pressed Nannie fondly to his heart, bade her farewell, and joined Captain Brown on board the "Maid of Carrick." Nannie sat down and watched the boat until it became a speck on the horizon, and then retraced her way sadly to Girvan.

The sun was setting in golden glory behind the heath-covered mountains of Arran, when the smugglers cast anchor in Brodick's bonny bay. The light breeze of easterly wind which had wafted them from Carrick, died away as the sun set, and the waters of the bay seemed liked a polished mirror, in which the evening star silently contemplates her silvery radiance.

Leaving Munro in the charge of the smack, Glentig, Brown, and Gordon lowered the boat and rowed ashore, to apprize Duncan Currie of their arrival. Duncan's house stood beneath the shelter of a huge oak, at the entrance of Glen Rosa. The Highlander never engaged in the illicit distillation of whisky personally, but for years he had acted as the accredited agent for the Carrick smugglers and the Highland distillers, to the entire satisfaction of both parties.

'Come awa', Captain Brown,' exclaimed Duncan courteously, as he opened the door and admitted him and his companions; 'I wad hae been in bed langsyne, but I fully expected ye the nicht. I hope ye hae a great order for me. Donald M'Gregor was tellin' me, to-day, he has a rare drap o' speerits on hand.'

Captain Brown briefly related the incidents of the last few days, and the despicable, mean, traitorous part Chapeldonnan had acted, and then informed him of the part he wished him to play, in working out his revenge.

'Here are a few bottles, Duncan, o' medicine I boucht frae Mr Crawford, at the heid o' the Kirkbrae, an' recollect, put a gill o' this into every keg ye fill, an' I'll see ye decently paid for yer trouble.'

'Ha, ha, ha!' roared Duncan, rubbing his hands, and dancing through the room, 'I'll no' tak' a single farthing for this job. If I dae, may the coin blister my fingers. This will be the best spree ever happened since I was appointed gauger for Arran. If ye manage yer job richt, Captain, I'll put yer next cargo on board free."

How long Duncan would have run on in this style, it is hard to say, had not Mrs Currie opened the door and asked if he was gaun gyte.

Supper being now served up, the smugglers set to with a will, and did ample justice to the fresh fish, eggs, and butter set before them, which was duly washed down with a steaming tumbler of toddy, and then they returned to their boat, and slept soundly until the sun was dancing on the water of the bay.

Leaving the smugglers to get their cargo on board, let us return to Chapeldonnan. After leaving the 'Ship,' in place of repairing to church, he proceeded homewards. Willingly would he have paid Captain Thomson a visit, but he was fearful of being seen in communication with the coastguard. On Monday morning, however, he was early astir and back in Girvan. After learning that Brown, Glentig, and Munro had put to sea, he proceeded to the Star Inn, and sent a boy of Mrs Clauchers over to the coastguard station to inform the Captain that he wished to speak with him on business of importance. In a short time the messenger returned, accompanied by the Captain, who was immediately shown into the room, where Chapeldonnan was anxiously waiting for him. Ordering in a dram, the door was carefully shut, and the laird of Chapeldonnan and the Captain began to make their arrangements for the capture of Brown and his confederates.

CHAPTER VII.

KIRKOSWALD, where Burns spent the eighteenth summer of his brief career, lies north of Girvan scarcely eight miles; and the distance between the Howe Port, where Brown was to land his cargo, from either of the former places, is only a few miles. Supposing, therefore, Burns and his companions had to walk to the place of rendezvous, it would, in those days, have been regarded only as an evening's recreation. Now, a perfumed exquisite will wait an hour or two on a train before he fatigues himself walking four miles ; and, of course, the lower class must ape the upper, and it is nothing astonishing to see a great hulking fellow, of twenty years of age, sleeping on a seat for two hours before he would run the risk of hurting his health by walking six miles.

Burns and his youthful companions, who were all more or less interested in smuggling, had no occasion to walk far, for it was only a *step*—as they called it—to the Maidenheads, then and now the abode of a hardy race of fishermen, where they easily procured a boat, and ran down along the coast to Girvan in little more than an hour.

Scarcely had they arrived at the Ship Inn, where they received an enthusiastic welcome from Nannie, when the Laird of Changue made his appearance, and the whole party sat down to an excellent supper, served in Miss Brown's best style—as the newspaper paragraphs say about all jollifications, good, bad, and indifferent.

When the cloth was removed, Tam Graham of the Shanter rehearsed some of his strange adventures over the bottle ; and amongst others, the story which formed the basis of the immortal tale of 'Tam o' Shanter.'

In this convivial manner the evening was spent, until it was considered time to start for the Howe Port, the place appointed to meet Brown.

Leaving the "Ship" by the back door, they crossed Girvan Water, skirted along the shore by Knockavalley and the Ladies' Loch, and reached the vicinity of the Howe Port by eleven o'clock.

In the meantime about a dozen of the coastguards, well armed with pistols and cutlasses, had arrived at Chapeldonnan, where the Laird was duly instructing them in the tactics to be pursued.

'Neither you nor yer men, Captain, maun show yer face till the last keg is brought ashore,' observed the Laird, as he issued his final instructions, 'for they're as cunning as foxes, and if they observed the least appearance o' danger they wad up sails and aff to sea, and deil kens when we wad see them again. Lie doon quietly aback o' a bent knowe until ye see me striking a licht for my pipe wi' my steel and flint, and then swoop doon on them like eagles.'

Promising to observe the Laird's instructions to the letter, Thomson led his men by a circuitous route to the sea-side, and selecting a spot favourable for observation, scanned the sea for the approach of the doomed smugglers.

It was the month of June, as we formerly observed, and although it was eleven o'clock at night, the roseate tints of the departed sun yet lingered in the north-west, and objects were discernible at a considerable distance.

'Yonder she comes at last,' said Thomson, speaking in a low voice to his men. 'Now, lads, be steady and clever, and I have not the least doubt but this night's work will lead to the promotion of ye, every man. Recollect every revenue officer from Stranraer to Greenock have their eyes on us, for it's well-known Brown and his crew are the most successful smugglers on the West Coast of Scotland. See, they're lowering their sails; be firm, do your duty like men, and wait for Chapel-donnan's signal.'

While Captain Thomson was addressing his men, the smugglers had cast anchor in the Howe Port, and were busy preparing to land their cargo.

'Monro, sprinkle the kegs again wi' the whisky,' cried Captain Brown, as he lowered himself into the small boat, 'Noo hand me doon a keg, an' I'll awa' ashore and see oor frien' Chapeldonnan.'

As the Laird saw Brown leave the smack, and row ashore, he rubbed his hands joyfully, and kept muttering to himself, 'Twa huner an' fifty pound, what a nicht's wark! An' revenge for the insults I received at Kirkdandie into the bargain. Weel dune, Captain Brown,' he exclaimed, rushing forward and extending his hand, which, however, the Captain seemed not to notice, as he busied himself securing the boat. 'I needna speir if ye hae secured a guid cargo,' continued Chapeldonnan, 'for the aroma coming frae the keg in the boat's delightfu.'

'It's as guid as ever was distilled in Glen Rosa,' observed the skipper of the 'Maid of Carrick' quietly. 'Hae ye the cash wi' ye?'

'Ay, here it's, lad, every penny,' said Chapeldonnan, pulling out his pocket book, and placing the notes in Brown's hand. 'Ye may count them if ye like.'

'Nae occasion to be sae particular wi' a friend,' observed

Brown, as he quietly deposited the money in an inside breast pocket, from which he took a brace of pistols and stuck them in his belt. 'Ye see, Laird, we maun mak' room for the siller,' observed Brown, smiling grimly.

Chapeldonnau neither relished the smile nor the action, and for the first time it struck him forcibly that if Brown suspected his treachery it might cost him his life, however, he observed after a pause, 'Oh, certainly, Captain! certainly—but ye'll better hurry the cargo ashore, seeing ye're paid for't.'

'Oh it will be landed time enough. I dinna see ony carts here yet,' observed Brown, looking around him.

'Never fash yer thum aboot carts, Captain. Land it on the beach an I'll see it taen hame.'

'A' richt, Laird; yer wull's my pleasure,' cried Brown, as he jumped into the boat and shoved her off.

In the greatest of mental anxiety the Laird of Chapeldonnan paced to and fro along the beach, until the last keg was landed, then advancing to where Brown, Glentig, and Munro, were standing, he rubbed his hands gleefully, and said he thought they micht hae a blaw o' the pipe, and a dram, seeing their nicht's wark was safely ower.

'Wi' a' my heart, Laird,' said Brown, pulling a flask from his pocket and handing it round.

Chapeldonnan drank success to the smugglers of Carrick, then pulled out his steel and flint, and began to strike a light.

Scarcely had he done so when Captain Thomson rushed with a yell down on the smugglers. In a moment they were surrounded, and Captain Thomson cried exultingly, 'Gentlemen, you're my prisoners, in the King's name!'

'For what, sir, are we your prisoners?' demanded Brown sternly.

'For what, ye scoundrel,' reiterated Thomson, in an indignant tone; 'for carrying on a contraband trade. How dare you have the audacity to ask such a question, and the evidence of your guilt lying on the beach?'

'If I have brought over anything contraband of the revenue laws of the country, then I'm your prisoner, Thomson; but beware of how you act in reference to a man carrying on a lawful trade,' said Brown firmly.

'Is it lawful, sir, to bring from Arran a cargo of whisky,

and dispose of it, that has never paid a halfpenny to the excise?' asked Thomson, burning with passion.

'No!' answered Brown, laughing, as he observed the Laird of Changue, acompanied by Burns and his friends from Kirk-oswald coming up. 'An' if ye find a gill o' whisky in ony o' the barrels lying there, then march me off to "Stumpy;" but recollect, Captain Thomson, if ye incarcerate me for following a lawful occupation, I'll strip that coat aff yer back.'

'An' what's in them, sir?' demanded Thomson in a quieter tone.

'Ask Chapeldonnan, they belang to him,' said Brown, playing with the butt of one of the pistols in his belt.

CHAPTER VIII.

HAD it not been for the sense of smell, Chapeldonnan would have suspected he was duped; but the very air he breathed was strongly impregnated with the alcoholic fragrance given off by the kegs lying on the beach. The same idea flashed through the mind of Thomson and Chapeldonnan at the same moment—Brown wishes to gain time until an overpowering number of his associates arrives, and then he will set us at defiance. The arrival of Changue, one of the most determined smugglers on the Carrick coast, strengthened this opinion, and the parley would have been ended at once by making the crew prisoners, but none of them cared about advancing on men so well armed, especially on Brown, whose right hand rested on the butt of the pistol in his belt.

'You hear, Chapeldonnan, what Brown says, that you know what the kegs contain,' observed Thomson.

'They smell sae strongly o' whisky that they inform on themsel's,' answered Chapeldonnan.

'Yet you know perfectly well, Laird, there's no' a drap o' whisky in them,' said Brown, looking sternly at him.

'No' a drap o' whisky in them,' repeated Chapeldonnan in a strange voice; 'an' dae ye mean to tell me I dinna ken the smell o' whisky, Brown?'

'Ye should, for ye hae drank mony a barrel o't. But when we were getting the peppermint water, which ye ordered, oot o' the hold, Monro spilt a drap o' speerits, that he had for his

private use, amoug the kegs, an' that's what ye fin' the smell
o'. But ye werena fou at the time, Laird, ye gied the order,
therefore ye maun hae perfect guid mind o't.'

'And do you mean to affirm, Captain Brown, that the kegs
lying there contain only peppermint water?'

'Nothing else, I can assure ye, Mr Thomson. The Laird
told me iu the inn that he had discovered a grand market for
that article in Glasca, and it seems the water o' Glen Rosa is
better adapted for that purpose thau ony we hae in the west——'

'The villain's drunk!' exclaimed Chapeldonnan fiercely,
interrupting Brown. 'Is there a man here believes him? But
I'll curst sune see whether it's peppermint water or no'.' As
he said this he struck one of the kegs savagely with his foot,
knocking the end of it completely iu, and the next moment the
fragrance of peppermint prevaded the air around them. A loud
derisive peal of laughter burst from the assembled smugglers.

Scarcely had it subsided, when Thomson, fuming with
rage and mortification, wheeled round fiercely on Chapeldonnan,
for he now regarded the whole as a plot to hold him up to
ridicule and contempt, and exclaimed savagely —'Villain, was
it for this you brought me here? If you were not such a
contemptible wretch, I would give you the contents of that.'
As Thomson said this he held the muzzle of his pistol so close
to Chapeldonnan's head that instinctively he sprang backwards,
tripped over one of the kegs, and fell heavily among the
barrels giving only a faint groan.

'Let the carrion lie there and rot,' shouted Thomson, who
now felt a thousand times more embittered against Chapeldonnan, for his supposed treachery, than what he did towards
the smugglers. 'Come, lads, follow me!'

'Ye'll better wait, Captain Thomson, au' see whether the
Laird's deid or leevin',' said Brown.

'If he's dead he will save the Ayr hangman the trouble of
stringing him up. Come, men, he's among his friends, and
they can look after him.'

'Are ye no' for a taste o' the peppermint before you gang,
Captain?' sneered Changue, as he passed where he stood
laughing. 'It's the best manufactured by Currie & Co., Glen
Rosa.'

'We'll meet again, Changue.'

'I houp sae, Captain. Gude-nicht.'

' This is the worst night's work ever I made since I joined the service, and the sooner I'm removed from this district the better, for between the fishers and weavers of Girvan I'll not get walking the streets.' This prediction proved true, for as soon as he appeared the following morning at ' Stumpy,' some one bawled out ' Captain Peppermint!'

As soon as Thomson and his men disappeared, Burns stepped forward and gazed into the face of Chapeldonnan, but seemingly he was dead, and he communicated his fears to the smugglers.

' I wudna put a han' to him,' cried Changue, 'if the tide was within a yard o' his ugly carcase.'

' Nor I either ! ' exclaimed Glentig. ' He's dune his best to ruin us a'.'

' I'm aware of that,' answered Burns; ' but the wretch is either dead or dying, and I could not rest in my bed if he was left to perish here.' As he said this he raised him up to a sitting posture, and examined the wound in the back part of the head. ' This is sad work, Mr Brown,' cried Burns, feelingly; ' Come here and help me.'

' We're no' to blame, Robin, supposing he wad never gie a kick,' observed Brown, as he helped Burns to tie a napkin round his head. This done he applied his flask, containing something stronger than peppermint, to his lips, which had the effect of restoring him to consciousness. Opening his eyes he looked hard at Brown and demanded his money. ' Puir body !' said Brown, mockingly, ' he hisna recovered his senses yet.'

' Gie me my twa huner and fifty pounds, Brown.'

' I'll gie ye the contents o' that,' said Brown in a low voice, ' if ye speak anither word. Look around ye; ye're frien's are awa hame, an' if it wusna for the sake o' the young man that's here, ye wad never leave the Howe Port alive—ye low, sneakin', mean, unprincipled villain. Noo, be off, before waur happens ye.'

Chapeldonnan looked round on the lawless group, and, without speaking another word, staggered homewards. Our tale is nearly told. A short time after the incidents narrated, Captain Thomson petitioned to be removed to another part of the coast, and, after his removal, Jamie Gordon returned to Girvan, and was united to Miss Brown in marriage. Since or before there never was such a merry wedding in the ' Ship.'

Burns and a number of his companions came to it from

Kirkoswald, and was highly amused by Jock Saunders singing the 'Crow,' and Charlie Johnston's recitation of the 'Duck's march over the flushes.' Unconsciously in such scenes the greatest son of Scotia was prepared for the dignified position in which, at last, his country proudly placed him. Changue's lovely daughter, Nannie, and the Laird of Mununcion were also present, when Miss Brown was given away in marriage by her brother, and, notwithstanding the size of the laird's feet, Burns declared he danced charmingly. Glentig swore the youthful bard kissed Nannie more than once on the back stair, but knowing Burns' aversion to such practices we are led to believe Glentig was 'tight.'

Chapeldounan recovered the effects of his fall, but he took the loss of his siller so sadly to heart that he got on the spree at next Kirkdandie Fair, through vexation at seeing Brown driving such a good trade, and died of the blues—the people knew nothing about *delirium tremens* in those days.

Changue lived to fight many a hard battle at Kirkdandie, and to hear his grandson sing

'Behind yon hills, where Stinchar flows,
'Mang moors and mosses many, O.'

THE GREY STONES OF GARLAFFIN.

CHAPTER I.

BALLANTRAE, or, as the name signifies, the 'town on the shore,' has been for centuries the abode of a fearless, hardy race of fishermen, and, until recently, of smugglers. It is built at the confluence of the Stinchar with the ocean. The parish is intersected by three glens, unsurpassed for wild picturesque beauty in the West of Scotland—the Stinchar, Tig, and App. The former is a lonely mountain stream, and the principal river in the district. It has its rise in the far off moors of the parish of Barr, on the farm of Black-Roo. After a rapid race of thirty miles through the most magnificent mountain scenery, it mingles its pellucid waters with the sea. From its rise to its confluence, it affords to every lover of nature unmingled pleasure. This is the stream to which Burns alludes in his popular ballad,

'Behind you hills, where Lugar flows.'

Lugar was substituted for Stinchar as more poetical, but, with all due deference to Burns, Stinchar seems the best name of the two.

Let the denizen of the city, who has a day or twos liberty to roam where he pleases, come and sit on the ruins of Ardstinchar Castle, and gaze around him on the swelling sea, bosky dells, enriched by every species of fern, and lofty hills. We'll guarantee that his vision will be in no manner obscured by the smoke incidental to the crowded marts of men. If not pleased with the view from this point, let him ascend Benivaird, at the head of Glen App. The view from this mountain is truly magnificent, commanding, as it does, the whole Firth of Clyde, with the Arran Hills, the Paps of Jura, Argyleshire, the Mull of Cantyre, the Isle of Rathlin, the Garron Head, the Mountains of Morn, the high lands in Cumberland, and the Isle of Man.

If he wishes to make altars of the mountains and the ocean, this is the spot. Nor is it difficult to reach. From the commercial capital of Scotland, you can sail direct to Ballantrae, per 'Albion,' every week, for two or three shillings; or, not liking that route, you can have rail and coach for little more; and those who have travelled the road between Girvan and Ballantrae will agree with the writer of these traditions, that it is a drive capable of stirring the deepest emotions of all who love the sublime and beautiful. Scarcely have you left Girvan when your attention is arrested by the sea-mews singing anthems o'er the altars of the main, perched upon Skart Rock; while looming to westward is Ailsa Craig—or, as it is more familiarly called, Paddy's-Milestone. The next turn of the road opens up Ardmillan Bay, and you are ready to exclaim—

> Oh! could the weary find a spot
> Like this, so passing fair,
> Life's e'ening sun wad never set
> Envelop'd in despair;
> But Hope would spring within their hearts,
> As bright as parting day,
> That rolls like molten streams of gold
> Across Ardmillan Bay.

But we must hurry on, as we have to attend an assignation at the 'Grey Stones of Garlaffin.'

It was a beautiful evening in Autumn, towards the latter end of the last century, when a young, beautiful girl might have been seen leaving one of the low thatched cottages in the Foreland, and tripping along in the direction of the Druid's Stones. Before she reached them, however, the moon had risen, like a burnished shield, over the tops of the eastern hills, presaging a good day for the hardy fishermen to-morrow. Having arrived at her destination, Mary sat down on a moss-covered stone, and gazed anxiously around her, as if expecting some one. Across the lovely valley of the Stinchar she could trace the dim outlines of the ruins of Ardstinchar, for many generations the abode of the Kennedys of Bargany. Falling into a musing mood, her active fancy re-peopled the hoary ruin, lighted its hall, and, in imagination, she listened to the minstrels recite and sing the daring deeds of its mighty lords.

'Dearest Mary, I am afraid I have kept you waiting and wearying here alone; but, really, it was unavoidable.'

'I never got sic a start in a' my life,' exclaimed Mary, as she took the outstretched hand of the young sailor, and shook it warmly.

'Sit down again, Mary, I have something to tell you about Knockdaw.'

'I hate, Bryce, to hear his name mentioned. He was ower at the Foreland last week, and it seems he has taken such a violent interest in my education that naething will sair him but send me to some fine lady's seminary.'

'Well, as I was coming here to-night he crossed my bows, and I could not steer clear of him for some time—that's what detained me.'

'Weel, what is he up to noo?'

'Oh! it seems his cellars are getting empty, and as he does not wish to support the coast-guard and excise—a lot of lazy hounds, he says, he wished me to supply him as reasonably as possible.'

'I warn ye, Bryce, to hae naething to dae wi' him. If ye hae ony respect for yoursel', or ony love for me, have no commerce wi' the ill-looking tyke,' cried Mary, passionately, springing to her feet and looking anxiously around her.

'Compose yourself, dearest Mary,' said the young man, in a soft, soothing tone of voice. 'Do you think I did not perceive the drift of the lubberly villain? I told him I was doing nothing in that line at present, but as soon as I could make a safe run I would keep him in mind, and so I parted from him.'

'That was wise, for notwithstanding his professions o' friendship, I hae no faith in Knockdaw.'

As Mary said this, the lovers moved away from the Druid's Stones, along the bauks of the stream, in the direction of Ballantrae.

'So you have no faith in Knockdaw, my pretty Mary,' muttered a man who rose slowly up from his crouching position among the grey moss-covered stones and looked savagely after the lovers as they walked away arm in arm. 'She hates me and fears me, and the brave, beardless captain of the "Speedwell" calls me a lubberly villain. I was strangely tempted to give him the contents of that as a remembrance of me;' as he said this, he pulled a heavy pistol from his breast and examined it, smiling grimly as he did so.

In place of proceeding homewards, Knockdaw, after leaving

the Grey Stones of Garlaffin, repaired to the village inn, where
his horse was put up, and with a tact, not unworthy of a
modern diplomatist, entered readily into the rough humour
of the fishermen, who frequented the publican's commercial
room.

The reader is not to suppose that in those days few gentlemen
would visit such an obscure village as Ballantrae. In arriving
at this conclusion, he would make a most egregious mistake.
A hundred people passed through it then for every one now.
When it is borne in mind that steamers and railways were undreamed of, and that the only route, between Ireland and
Scotland, for lords, ladies, and gentlemen, was *via* Portpatrick,
Stranraer, Ballantrae, Girvan, and Ayr, he will instantly change
his opinion. Scarcely a week passed without regiments of
soldiers, gangs of sailors, and civilians of every grade, from
the gipsy to the rich pedlar—the latter supplied the guidwife
with the newest fashions, and the guidman with whatever was
stirring in the country. After escorting Mary Ferguson home,
the Captain of the 'Speedwell' strolled along the beach until
he reached the Stinchar, then ascended the bank of the stream,
until he arrived at the bridge, seated himself on the parapet and
watched the moonbeams dancing on the water, and the travel-
lers who passed. He was unconscious of the flight of time, for
he was busily engaged at a piece of work common to the youthful in every age and clime—building castles in the air; and a
superb structure it was, Mary, of course, reigning in queenly
style in its hall—when a man abruptly asked ' Do you belong
to Ballantrae ?'

' I know it well, and I think I know you too—is your name
M'Creadie ?'

The stranger hesitated a moment ere he replied, but gazing
keenly at the frank face of the Captain, he answered in the
affirmative.

' I thought so. It's many years since I saw you, but boys
always remember the faces with which they have been familiar.
I know one man in the clachan who will be delighted to see
you.'

' To whom do you refer ?'

' Jamie Ferguson, in the Foreland.'

' How strange! It was about him I was going to inquire.
Ay, and Jamie's still living yet'—the last sentence was said in

a musing tone, more to himself than to the Captain of the
'Speedwell.'

'How long is it since you left here, M'Creadie?'

'Fourteen years this very night. The revenue officers
were after me about that cursed smuggling affair in which
Willie M'Whirter was so seriously injured. I did what I
could to throw the land sharks off the scent of the booty, and
so got myself into hot water—'

'I have heard Jamie Ferguson relate many a time how
nobly you behaved; but,' here he lowered his voice to a
whisper, 'Was the Laird of Knockdaw at that time supposed
to have acted treacherously?'

'Curse him! ay; but I have a pickle prepared for him that
will make him start some of these days; but it's a dry job
standing speaking here after a long journey.'

'Pardon my forgetfulness!' exclaimed Bryce, springing
from his seat on the bridge, 'but the sight of your face, and the
joy I experienced when I saw the man who many a time took
me to sea with him when I was a boy, must be my apology.'

'What's your name?'

'Bryce Girvan.'

'My gallant little Captain, as I used to call ye—is it possible? Why, I'm blowed if I'm not as happy to meet you as
I would be if running a prize into harbour.'

Conversing in this manner they approached the inn, but just
as they were about to enter, Kennedy of Knockdaw passed out.
Being far gone in drink, however, he paid no attention to the
traveller.

'That's your old friend, M'Creadie,' observed the Captain
in an undertone.

'I knew his ugly figurehead in a moment. But tell me this,
Bryce, what became of the lassie or child Ferguson picked up
in the bay?'

'Were you here at that time? Ferguson told me you left
the day before that memorable event.'

'Yes, Ferguson is quite correct; I left Ballantrae, but
stayed all night in the Benmane Cave, waiting for a little of the
needful to carry me out of the locality, and hereby hangs a tale
which will surprise you and alarm the Laird of Knockdaw.
But I will not relate it here.'

CHAPTER II.

"Come, sit thee down, my bonny lass ;
Come, sit thee down by me, love ;
And I will tell thee many a tale,
Of the dangers of the sea, love."

'BRAVO, Drynan! Sing it out, man; it's only the skipper o' the "Speedwell" an' a freen o' his,' cried Tam Coulthard, the captain and sole owner of the 'Jenny and Nancy' of Ballantrae. But Drynan was put out a little by the entrance of the expert smuggler, Bryce Girvan, and the keen, sharp, weather-beaten appearance of his companion, and would sing no more.

'Bring a pint o' your best whisky, lassie; and, messmates, permit me to introduce to you my friend, and your comrade for many a year—Jack M'Creadie, of the Shellknowes.'

'Is it possible? Gie's a grup o' yer fin! Od! but Kate Maclure will be the proud lass to see ye!' These were the exclamations which greeted Jack on all sides as he took the seat of honour at the head of the table.

As the night wore on, many were the strange tales told of hairbreadth escapes from waves and excisemen; but as M'Creadie wished to spend an hour with his old friend Ferguson, he had to bid them good night, and leave M'Ilraith in the midst of a graphic account of the wreck of the 'Monte Video.'

No sooner did Captain Girvan get M'Creadie in tow for the Foreland, than he again reverted to the Laird of Knockdaw.

'Well, it's a long yarn,' began M'Creadie, 'but as the night is good, and I wish to have a ramble along the old familiar beach, I will gratify your curiosity. But, before I introduce my story, I must make a few observations. You must know that the Lairds of Bennane and Knockdaw are Kennedys, and nearly related—David Kennedy having disappeared somewhat mysteriously, leaving a daughter, a child about three years of age, to heir his estate. As there was no will to be found, Knockdaw conceived the idea of annexing it to his own; and as he was the nearest of kin, in the event of the child's death, it was his legally. To facilitate his diabolical project, he, under the pretence of great friendship, became the child's guardian; but she had not been many weeks at Knockdaw until she sickened and died, and was duly interred in the family vault.'

H

'Thank God!' fervently ejaculated Bryce Girvan. 'Do you know, I was trembling with fear lest the child should turn out to be Mary Ferguson.'

'Oh! I see how the land lies; but to resume my story.

'This night, fourteen years ago, I was lying in the Bennane Cave, while the coastguard were searching for me in Ballantrae. Kate knew where I was, and after sunset paid me a visit, bringing me a change of linen and a little money. It was a beautiful night—just such another as this—and the hours passed unheeded until day began to break, when we were forced to part amidst showers of briny tears. It was anything but a dry affair, I can assure ye. Poor thing, I'm glad she's living and well.' As Jack said this, he drew the back of his hand across his eyes, and spoke rather hoarsely.

'Kate had scarcely left half an hour when I saw two men approaching the cave. One of them had a large bundle, which he carried carefully in his arms. As they advanced I retreated into a dark recess of the cavern, and as they were only a few yards from me, I heard every word they said.

'"This is confoundedly strange, M'Cord," observed the tallest of the two, who stood muffled up in his cloak, peering through the grey mist of morning over the bay. "Sloan promised to have that old leaky craft of his round from the Whilk by this time, and I see no appearance of him yet. By St Cuthbert, if you give me the brat I'll hurl her over the rocks into the sea."

'"Have patience, Knockdaw; Sloan will not disappoint ye."

'"Have patience!" exclaimed Knockdaw, savagely. "The public think she is dead and buried at any rate, so give me the child and I'll nurse her." As Knockdaw said this he advanced and held out his hands.

'"Stand off, Laird Kennedy, or I'll do you a mischief. Thank God, there's the boat."

'"Did you give her the laudanum?"

'"Yes, yes. Let us hurry down to the beach."

'Stupefied with horror, I gazed after them until they reached the verge of the sea; then I saw Knockdaw dip the child in the waves, throw her on board the crazy boat, and shove her off. Merciful God, what was I to do! If I returned to Ballantrae and informed on the villains, I had every prospect of ending my days on a cotton plantation on the banks of the Mississippi.

Knockdaw might affirm that it was a daring falsehood, fabricated by a lawless fellow to blast his character, as he was known to be friendly to the revenue officers. So the idea was no sooner formed than it was dismissed.

'Meantime the ebb and a pirl of easterly wind carried the boat and its helpless charge rapidly from the shore; but never will I forget with what gratitude I thanked God when I saw Ferguson's boat round the Foreland, and make straight for the wreck, as I have no doubt he supposed it to be. You know the sequel better than I do.'

The Captain of the 'Speedwell' had listened with breathless attention to M'Creadie's narrative, and his heart was far too good not to rejoice at the brilliant prospects it opened up to Mary, although, as the heiress of Bennane, it raised, he thought, an insuperable barrier between them. 'Well, this is the most extraordinary yarn ever I heard spun. Ferguson, of course, picked up the boat and towed her here; but it was always supposed by the fishermen that the ship to which she belonged had been lost on the west coast of Ireland. She was considered to have been a long time tossed about, as the child was half-dead with wet and cold.'

'The effects of the dip in the bay and the laudanum,' observed Jack.

'Just so. I see it all now as plain as a marlinspike; but at the time such was the supposition.'

'And quite nat'ral, too.'

'Well, Ferguson had lost his own little Mary a short time before this strange occurrence, and Bessie took to the little waif of the waves at once. Indeed, she maintains to this day there was something *providential* in it.'

'Then she is living yet?'

'Living and well,' responded the Captain; 'I parted with her not two hours ago.'

'I thought as much, from your impatience; but it's quite nat'ral at your time of life,' said Jack, with a sigh.

'But you have never told me how you left the Bennane Cave?'

'Well, after I saw the child picked up I left it with a lighter heart, and began to beat up for Girvan, keeping along the shore as closely as I could sail, for I was afraid to keep the road, and this saved me a wearisome journey.'

'How?'

'I had just got the length of Ardmillan Cave, when feeling more down-hearted than weary, I sat down to enjoy the weed. To tell you the truth, Kate was giving me a considerable amount of uneasiness, and I sat smoking and thinking, until a tight looking craft, that was hugging the land, sent a boat ashore and invited me to come aboard and have dinner with the Captain of the "Spitfire." I objected, but they urged me so strongly that I was glad to comply. Although I was unaware of it, the American war of independence had commenced, and, as the navy needed hands, I was pressed into the service. After cruising on the West Coast of Ireland some days, the "Spitfire" bore away to Dublin, and I was drafted on board the "Shannon." At the memorable action between her and the "Chesapeake" I had the privilege of hauling down the saucy Yankee's bunting, for which I was made captain of the fore-top. Since, I have been round the world, and at last got discharged with a good character and a well-filled purse, and here I am.'

By this time they had arrived at Ferguson's house, in the Foreland, and as Drynan had informed Kate of Jack's arrival, she was waiting and wearying to see him. The meeting was a joyful one; and as M'Creadie had been a great favourite before leaving, one after another dropped in to see him, so that it was morning before he went to rest.

Knockdaw left Ballantrae and proceeded homewards, with his mind filled with anything but agreeable reflections. The very sight or name of the young lady he had so grossly wronged, tended at all times to disturb his equanimity, and fill his mind with vague fears for the future. Mentally, he resolved to have her removed from the locality, but how it was to be accomplished, as yet, was not clearly defined. When in Ballantrae he had not been idle. He had learned, through one of his emissaries, that the 'Speedwell' was to sail for a cargo of contraband goods on an early day, and he determined to use every means in his power to have the energetic Captain apprehended by the Government officers. 'But it would be better,' he soliloquised, 'if I could induce Comyn to scuttle his ship. I'll see what money can do, after I have consulted with M'Cord.'

In this amiable disposition he reached Knockdaw and summoned his hoary accomplice into his service.

Tam M'Cord was a man now well advanced in years. He had entered Kennedy's service young, and had committed a *faux pas* before he was long in it, which had given the unprincipled Laird a complete ascendency over his less astute companion—for such he had become, although a servant. As they advanced in years—they were about an age—they progressed in vice, and it was nothing strange for M'Cord to set his master at defiance. During a series of years they had committed so many mean actions in company that they both feared and hated each other.

'I was at the clachan to-night, M'Cord,' said Knockdaw, in that silly, idiotic style peculiar to drunkards.

'Did you bring me here to tell me that?'

'No, you impudent scoundrel, I did not.'

'Well, whatever you have got to say, be quick about it, for I have a stranger to attend to.'

'A stranger, M'Cord; you astonish me. Who the —— has deigned to visit Knockdaw?'

'One you must welcome.'

'Tell me at once who he is, or I'll throttle ye?'

'Jamie Colville.'

'The lawyer from Ayr, who made himself so busy when Katherine died? I wish to —— she had. But it was all your fault, M'Cord. I must go and see him. You may swear there is mischief a-brewing.'

'Better see him in the morning. I can say you are unwell and gone to bed.'

'I'll take your advice for once, M'Cord. Away, and tell him whatever lie comes uppermost.'

CHAPTER III.

JACK M'CREADIE and the Captain of the 'Speedwell' met on the following morning by appointment; and as the 'Grey Stones of Garlaffin' was a spot but little frequented, they repaired thither to hold their conference. After looking at M'Creadie's tale from every point of view, it was considered best, in the meantime, to say nothing about it to either Mary or her foster parents. They had powerful reasons for this line of policy. Knockdaw, they reasoned, would move heaven and earth to screen himself and retain the property. He would have no difficulty in proving that Mary was buried long ago, for nearly half of the parishioners had attended the funeral. This done, it would not be hard to persuade the people that M'Creadie's story was a base fabrication, concocted between her lover—who was well known to be a smuggler—and a man who had to fly the country for a similar offence. 'I see rocks ahead,' observed M'Creadie, gravely, ' no matter how I view this ugly piece of work; but having turned it over in my mind for fourteen years, I'll tell thee, Captain, what I think would be our best mode of procedure. Let us go to-night to the Old Church and examine the family vault of the Kennedys of Bennane, and ascertain if the coffin of Katherine is in its place, and what it contains. Having satisfied ourselves on that head, we can summon the inhabitants, and prove the truth of my statements.'

'A noble idea, Jack,' exclaimed the Captain, ' and one which we must carry out at once.'

Returning to the village they spent the remainder of the day visiting friends; but towards evening they mysteriously disappeared, much to the chagrin of their numerous acquaintances, and bent their steps in the direction of the kirk.

The original church of Ballantrae was situated near the confluence of the Tig and the Stinchar. The ruins stand, or did lately, on the property of Garfar, about two miles from the sea. The church was granted to the monks of Crossraguel by the founder of that monastery, Duncan, Earl of Carrick, and confirmed to them by Robert I. and Robert III. The monks enjoyed the patronage tithes; and the other profits of the church belonged to the vicarage, which was established by the Bishop of Glasgow. Having arrived at the ruinous edifice, the two sat down in the shadow of the wall, and looked around them in silence. The night was calm and clear. Not a cloud obscured the brilliancy of the moon; and as her silvery radiance shone through the trees upon the last resting-place of many generations of rich and poor, they felt a solemn awe steal over them. Indeed, the mission which had brought them to such a place, at such an hour, induced anything but feelings of levity. In endeavouring to restore to a defenceless girl what was justly hers, they felt they had a sacred duty to fulfil, and they were determined to discharge it faithfully. To facilitate their purpose, M'Creadie had brought a lantern with him, and was busy engaged trimming it when their attention was arrested by approaching footsteps.

'There's some one coming this way,' said the Captain, in a scarcely audible voice; 'let us crouch down close behind this stone.'

Without replying, Jack M'Creadie followed his comrade's example, for now they could distinctly hear the voices of men in conversation.

'This is the place, Mr Colville; there's the vault of the Kennedys at the east corner,' said the one who apparently acted as guide.

'You have the keys with you, Ramsey, I suppose?'

'Yes, sir, and the light.'

'Well, let us proceed to work at once, for I'm quite impatient to test the truth of the anonymous note I received. If it holds true, Knockdaw may look out.'

'I can scarcely credit it, sir; but we can soon learn—this is the entrance.'

After trying a variety of keys, they found one which fitted the lock, and in a moment they both disappeared inside.

'Who can they be?' asked Captain Girvan, springing to his feet.

'How should I know? but evidently they are no friends of Knockdaw. Let's see what they're about,' said M'Creadie, as he peered through one of the loopholes peculiar to charnel houses. Captain Girvan followed his example.

In the centre of the place allotted to the dead stood the two strangers, both fashionably dressed. The tallest of the two might be about forty years of age; his companion was somewhat younger, with a frank expression of face and deep-set grey eyes. The other, who was evidently his superior, had a sharp, swarthy face, aquiline nose, restless black eyes, and stood gazing at three slabs, with rings attached to them, lying at his feet over the resting place of the dead.

These peculiarities of dress and features M'Creadie and the Captain had an ample opportunity of noting, as they stood with the light between them on the floor of the vault.

'Help me to lift these stones aside, Ramsey.'

Without speaking another word, they both bent down and carefully removed the slabs which covered the grave.

'Hold up the light; there, that will do. Here is the coffin of "Katherine Kennedy, aged three years and four months." How very particular Knockdaw has been! But what does it contain?'

'Have you the tools?'

'Yes, sir.'

'Well, set to work and raise the lid.'

Ramsey obeyed in silence, and in the course of a few minutes it was uncovered.

'Here's the child,' exclaimed Ramsey, dragging forth a large billet of oak, and throwing it on the floor.

'The infernal scoundrel,' exclaimed the Captain, involuntarily, who had watched the whole proceedings with intense anxiety through the iron grating.

Ramsey and Colville leaped nearly off their feet, the latter exclaiming—'Good heavens, did you not hear some one speak?'

'Yes, sir, and I fear we have been watched, for I could swear it was a human voice I heard.'

'You need not be alarmed, gentlemen,' said Captain Girvan, as he opened the door of the vault and stepped inside. 'You have only anticipated us in our work.'

'' What mean you, sir?' demanded Colville, sternly, as he stepped a pace back, and drew a pistol from his breast pocket.

'Simply that we're friends of the wronged heiress, and came here for the express purpose of doing what you have done.'

'You were many years of using the knowledge which you possessed,' said Colville, still keeping the muzzle of the pistol pointed towards the Captain.

'I might retort with equal propriety, and charge you with either negligence or want of knowledge; but here's my comrade has known it for fourteen years.'

'Ha! and what was the reason he kept his secret so long?'

'Jack,' said the Captain, addressing M'Creadie, 'you'll better rehearse to the gentlemen the tale you told me.'

Without any hesitation, M'Creadie commenced in a clear, manly voice, and related what the reader already knows. As he proceeded with his narrative, the group formed a picture that Rembrandt would have been delighted to paint. Mr Colville stood with his left foot resting on the wooden representative of the house of Bennane, bent forward in his anxiety to catch every word that fell from Jack's lips, while in his right hand he still retained the pistol. Ramsey stood by his side, with his keen grey eyes fixed on the face of the narrator. The Captain of the 'Speedwell' was standing opposite Mr Colville, with his right hand thrust into his left breast—for he never travelled at night without a brace of barkers. The lamp was languishing for want of being trimmed, and threw a sickly gloom on the damp, slimy walls, which gave them a most repulsive look.

When M'Creadie concluded his tale Mr Colville put up his pistol, and grasping M'Creadie warmly by the hand, he exclaimed, ' I am deeply your debtor, for, but for you, the discovery which we have made would have availed but little, as we would have been still ignorant of the fate of the child.'

' Thank God ! she's living and well,' exclaimed M'Creadie, fervently.

' Amen,' responded Mr Colville.

' Seeing we have been so explicit with you, I think, sir, you should inform us how you acquired any knowledge of an event that occurred so many years ago,' observed Mr Girvan.

' My tale is soon told. The Laird of Bennane and I were most intimate friends. He attached himself to the cause of Charles Edward, and, it is supposed, fell at the battle of Preston. He left no will that can be discovered. Upon the demise of his infant daughter, the property, of course, became Knockdaw's, and a suspicion that he had used foul play to obtain possession never once crossed my mind. Last week, however, I received an annoymous letter which stated that the heiress was not dead, and that the funeral was a mockery; that if I wished to assure myself of the truth of the writer's statement, I had only to come here and I would find, instead of a child, a block of wood in the coffin. It was such a wild, improbably-looking tale that I hesitated some time before I informed Mr Ramsey of the communication, but he took quite a different view of the affair. So we left Ayr and arrived at Knockdaw last night. The Laird came home late, and I did not see him ; so I started early this morning, telling M'Cord to inform his master that I had some business of importance to transact in Ballautrae, but that I hoped to return and see him in the course of a day or two. You know the rest.'

' Well, how do you intend to proceed now ? ' asked Captain Girvan, in an anxious voice.

'In the meantime, let us replace the wooden body in the coffin, and every one must keep secret our nocturnal visit to this place. We will separate before we enter Ballantrae; but to-morrow evening meet me and Ramsay at the "Grey Stones of Garlaffin," and I will inform you what I think is best to be done.'

Having replaced the wood in the coffin, and locked the door, they proceeded down the Stinchar in the direction of Ballantrae.

CHAPTER IV.

THE unexpected visit of Messrs Colville and Ramsey, and their sudden departure, had seriously annoyed Knockdaw and his accomplice in crime. Years had elapsed since they had con-jointly committed the foul deed that had placed Knockdaw in the possession of Bennane; still their consciences were as easily alarmed as if the crime had been committed yesterday. There was only one individual living, they thought, that knew the whole details of the conspiracy, and she was getting ad-vanced in years, and was still in his service; therefore they had no dread of Janet Baird, the housekeeper. In earlier years M'Cord had made love to her, as it was necessary to secure her aid in carrying out their plans regarding the infant heiress. As M'Cord was not a man given to marriage, he delayed the fulfilment of his promise to wed her from month to month and from year to year, and latterly he abandoned her altogether. It is said—'Hope deferred maketh the heart sick,' and the wisest man might have added—bitter too. If M'Cord had forgotten his promise, Janet had not; and as drowning men are said to catch at straws, so Janet had arrived at that time of life when women become terrified they are to remain in a state of single blessedness for ever, and she resolved to make her faithless swain fulfil his promise and marry her, or take steps secretly to work his ruin. Accordingly, she threw off her apron (a few days previous to the opening of this tale), donned her silk gown, and garnished her mutch with an enormous quantity of red ribbons, and held her way down to the great man's apartment. Janet neither stammered, blushed, nor bowed as she entered it, but, coolly taking a seat, bade M'Cord good morning.

'In the name o' everything that's gude, Miss Baird, whaur

are ye going this morning? I didna see ye sae well dressed syne the nicht ye attended Meg M'Kissock's bridal.'

'The next bridal I gang to maun be my ain—'

'A wise resolution, Miss Baird,' observed M'Cord, interrupting her; 'really I'm surprised a lass o' your appearance didna tak' a man lang syne.'

'I never got the chance, and a' through you, ye deceiving, black-hearted, lying villain,' exclaimed Janet, storming up.

'Whist! for gude's sake, whist, Miss Baird, the Laird will hear ye, and ye ken he likes quietness in the morning.'

'I carena a fig for the Laird!' cried Janet, snapping her fingers in his face; but the next moment she resorted to woman's strength and weakness, and began to sob bitterly. 'I hae seen the day, Mr M'Cord, when ye were glad to see me coming the way o' yer room. I wasna Miss Baird then, but "dear Janet, my pretty bird, and bonnie lassie;" but I'm cheaply set aside noo, and sairs me richt for lavishing my love on a man that disna care I was thrown ower Gamesloup.'

'I'm always glad to see ye, Janet. Sae dry yer bonnie een and listen to reason.'

'Weel, what are ye gaun to say?' asked Janet, looking at her lover through her tears.

'Ye see, dear, we're baith getting weel up in years——'

'I kenna about yer age, Mr M'Cord, but I'm no that auld but I could mak' a comfortable hame for ye yet.'

'Granted, my dawtie; but ye interrupted me before I had my say oot. As I was remarking, we're baith getting—or at least I am growing auld, and seeing we hae wanted the comforts ye were speaking aboot sae lang, I think it wad be baith improper and sinfu' to disturb the even tenor o' oor life noo.'

'Am I to understand, Mr M'Cord, that ye never intend to marry?'

'That's exactly the meaning o' my words, Miss Baird.'

'If ye "Miss Baird" me again, ye low, unprincipled vagabond, I'll tear yer ugly een oot.' As Janet advanced with the intention of putting her threat into execution, the door opened, and the Laird of Knockdaw stepped into the apartment.

Janet cast a look of scorn and hatred at her faithless swain, and hastily retreated to her room.

Bolting her door, she sat down at the table, and, in her

passion, penned the note which had brought Mr Colville to Ballantrae.

The morning after Colville left Knockdaw, the Laird held a long conference with M'Cord, and many were the conjectures hazarded as to the cause of his visit. Somehow they had a presentiment that it boded them no good. 'I think the best thing we can do is to set Comyn on Colville's trail. Send him here, and I'll give him instructions.'

M'Cord hastened to obey his master's commands, and in a short time returned in company with Comyn, who acted as the Laird's spy and emissary upon all occasions.

For some years past M'Cord had lost the confidence of the smugglers who frequented the port of Ballantrae and the Bay of Finnart, and as Comyn was an expert smuggler, and had every appearance of being an open-hearted, frank, fearless man, he was quite a favourite in the village.

'Comyn,' said the Laird, addressing him as soon as he entered his apartment, 'I wish you to do me a bit of service, for which I intend to reward you handsomely.'

'Is it of a dangerous nature?' asked Comyn, for he knew the Laird better than suppose he was going to give him much for doing little.

'No, but it will require all your tact to do it well. You must go to Ballantrae and learn the whereabouts of a Mr Colville. You may easily distinguish him by his dress, which is somewhat uncommon in this district. Kneebreeches of black silk velvet, and hose to match, a vest of the same material, and a short, fashionable, dark cloak; rather tall in stature, swarthy features, and dark eyes—that's the man. You must follow his movements; wherever he goes never lose sight of him for a single moment, but beware of attracting his attention, for he's as sharp as a hawk. Dog his footsteps until he retires for the night, and return here before you sleep. Now, go at once, and there's an earnest of my determination to pay you well.'

As the Laird said this he tossed Comyn his purse across the table. Comyn's eyes dilated with pleasure as he pocketed the money, for his ruling passion was avarice. To gratify his love of gold, he was willing to engage in the most reckless and unlawful enterprise.

Drinking a glass now and again, he loitered about the

Ballantrae Inn all day, seeing Mr Colville and Ramsey pass
out and in. As night set in, however, he observed them bend
their steps in the direction of the Stinchar, and thither he
followed them, until they reached the vicinity of the Parish
Church. Screened from observation by the trees, which grew
around it, he approached it cautiously, and saw Colville and his
companion enter it; but to Comyn's great astonishment, the
Captain of the 'Speedwell' and another man approached the
loopholes, before mentioned, and peered through them. He
now conjectured it was a smuggling affair, and that Knockdaw
had employed him to discover where the booty was hid; for,
strange as it may sound in the ears of our readers, one of the
best receptacles of smuggled goods in the parish was a vault
beneath the church. 'I can now perceive the cause of Knockdaw's unwonted liberality,' muttered Comyn, 'but if the knowledge is worth so much to him, it must be of value to me.' He
had just arrived, mentally, at this laudable conclusion, when
Captain Girvan and his companion disappeared inside. The
coast was now clear, so approaching the wickets he saw and
heard all with which the reader is already acquainted.

Comyn, having made the great discovery of Knockdaw's
villany, hastened down the Stinchar, cogitating all the way
how he should make the best use of his knowledge. At last
he resolved to extort from the Laird all the money he could,
securing to himself the liberty of either acting with or against
him, as circumstances would suggest.

By the time he reached the Laird's it was getting late, but
on announcing himself he was shown by M'Cord at once to
Knockdaw's apartment.

As the Laird and M'Cord listened to Comyn's tale they shook
with dismay. Until this moment, they had considered their
crime of outrage and wrong safe in their own keeping, but now
there was proof as clear and strong as holy writ against
them; and to complete their horror, Comyn was also cognizant
of their base treachery. The same thought swept instantane-
ously through Knockdaw and M'Cord's mind that, whatever
was the future consequences, he would have to be disposed of;
but he was a strong, powerful man, and if the attempt upon
his life miscarried, it might cost them theirs immediately.

'I need not say to you, Comyn, that, in the meantime, I
depend on you, as I would on my nearest friend, that you will

retain your knowledge of this affair closely to yourself,' said Knockdaw.

'That depends on how I'm paid, Laird,' observed Comyn.

A rapid glance passed between Knockdaw and M'Cord, which Comyn failed to perceive, so busily was he engaged computing how much he should ask for keeping his secret, or rather theirs.

'I'm aware of that, Comyn; and that I intend to pay you handsomely I think you had a convincing proof this morning.'

'Yes, that's true enough; but you see, Knockdaw, this is an important secret, and must be be paid for accordingly.'

'I pledge you my word you shall have no reason to reflect on my want of liberality to-morrow night; but it's now one o'clock, and as you have a good way to go I must bid you good-night. Take another glass of brandy and then start.'

Comyn started, but it was reluctantly. He had a long, lonely road before him, but the night was clear and good, and being well primed with brandy he journeyed bravely along. The cottage in which he resided was not in the village, and from Knockdaw there were two ways of reaching it. The shortest way led through a waste, thickly strewn with huge whinstone boulders and black frowning rocks, which seemed very pretty when the sun was shining, but at night they had a wild, weird-looking appearance. He had arrived nearly at the public road, and had commenced to clamber down the precipice which bounded it on the east, when he sprang suddenly off his feet and fell forward down the face of the bleak rock. The next moment the report of a pistol awoke the sleeping echoes, and died far away among the hills.

CHAPTER V.

IT was far advanced in the morning when the Laird of Knock-daw came from his chamber, and sat down to breakfast. The meal passed in silence, for he well knew the crisis of his fate had arrived, and unless he could dispose of Colville and his friends, as Comyn had been last night, utter ruin, and perhaps a shameful death, stared him in the face. These were the thoughts which occupied his mind as he tried to eat a little, but the excitement and excess of last night had completely destroyed his appetite. He felt the necessity of conferring with M'Cord, but somehow his nature revolted against it. It may seem strange, but after every additional crime they avoided each other more and more, and as they advanced in years their hatred of each other was proportionally increased. Perhaps they were taught by experience to justly estimate each other's worth.

As the Laird sat chewing the cud of bitter reflection the door opened and Mr M'Cord walked in and sat down. If death levels all distinctions, so does crime ; and Knockdaw saw and felt the truth of this observation as he looked askance at his servant.

'We have a more difficult job before us to-night than we had this morning,' observed Knockdaw, eyeing his servant and accomplice keenly.

'Not a bit, if we go about it as cautiously. At most there will be but four of them, and there are plenty of pistols here. I intend taking a few in my belt, and I suppose you will do the same. If they had left the selection of the place of meeting to you and me they could not have pleased me better. How easy it will be for us to secrete ourselves among the whin and broom which grow so luxuriantly among the grey stones of Garlaffin, and bring down our man as gracefully as you would a pheasant.'

'M'Cord, you have been drinking this morning, and recollect if we bungle this job to-night, it will cost us our lives,' said the Laird, in a sober manner.

'I could not help taking a drop, for I felt so nervous since I dropped Comyn over the crag into the sea.'

'He's safe enough, at any rate,' observed the Laird, shuddering, and looking anxiously round the room. 'Do you know, M'Cord, I think I have a touch of the *blues* myself—I never felt as queer in all my life. You'd better bring in the bottle.'

Leaving these confederates in crime to mature their plans, let us return to Ballantrae and ascertain how the other characters in the drama are passing their time.

Jack M'Creadie and Kate had retired for an hour or two to the ruins of Ardstinchar, where they had spent many a happy, joyous day—

> When earth appeared a blest abode,
> And life a long, bright, pleasant road.

Here Jack, with his arms around Kate's waist, renewed the vows of his youth, to which she listened as eagerly as she did fourteen years ago. Some of the ill-speaking gossips affirmed that she had never received the offer of a man, else she would not have waited so long on M'Creadie; but this was nothing but spleen, for it could have been easily attested that Drynan, the fisher, and Macilray, the blacksmith, both sought the hand of Miss Maclure in marriage, but had been courteously refused. We say *courteously;* for Katie, being a kind, good, wise girl, felt uncommonly to break the heart of the burly blacksmith. Of course, while Jack was sitting with his arms around her waist, he was informed of this and far more.

The 'Speedwell' was lying in the port ready to start on her perilous cruise, but the Captain was not on board. Ever since he heard the strange tale about Mary, his mind could settle to nothing. His crew remarked there was something wrong, but they never imagined there was a woman in the case. Their opinion was that Captain Girvan had only to court and win the greatest lady in the land. Indeed, as far as good looks, breeding, and bravery were concerned, he deserved nothing less, but these things do not go so much by merit as the length of the purse, and the Captain's money bags not being weighty enough to marry an heiress, he felt desponding and melancholy.

Mary and the Captain were walking arm-in-arm along the beach, picking up shells and carrying on a conversation in low tones, although there was no one near.

'I'm going to suppose a case, Mary, but it's only a supposition,' said the Captain, stooping down and lifting up a beautiful pebble; 'if you were becoming immensely rich, having a fine estate, and carriage, would you not regret wedding an obscure individual like me?'

'Bryce! what makes you ask such a strange question? Wha's gaun to leave me an estate or anything else? Ye should speak sensibly.'

'I didn't say, dearest Mary, any person was going to leave you an estate; I'm only supposing such a thing.'

'Weel, then, suppose naething aboot it, for neither station nor riches can or could ever change my affection for you.'

The Captain rewarded this declaration not by kissing her, for the bay was dotted with fishing boats, while Misses M'Hatteric and Simpson, two of the most celebrated gossips of the village, were pretending to water a web of linen they had out bleaching, but in reality they were watching the lovers; therefore he only pressed her hand and said—'Mary, this avowal will comfort me by night and by day when far from Ballantrae.'

'Wherever ye go, dear Bryce, my prayers will be duly offered up night and morning for your safety. And, oh! I beseech ye to abandon this perilous life, and settle doun to some peacefu' occupation.'

'Well, well, love, if this be a successful run I'll make it the last voyage in the "Speedwell."'

Colville and Ramsey spent the greater part of the day about the inn, but towards night they took their departure for the 'Grey Stones of Garlaffin.' They had scarcely reached the place of rendezvous when they were joined by Captain Girvan and M'Creadie. Although the day had been beautiful, towards evening it changed, and, as darkness set in, a strong breeze of westerly wind swept up the Stinchar, while large masses of clouds kept driving over the face of the moon, occasionally obscuring her altogether.

'I have come to the conclusion, my friends,' observed Mr Colville, 'that the best thing we can do is to proceed to Knockdaw to-morrow and make a prisoner of the Laird, charge him with the crime of obtaining possession of Bennane unlawfully, and with the abduction of the infant heiress.'

Before another word could be spoken, the party were suddenly startled by the report of a pistol, immediately behind where they stood sheltered by the broom and whin bushes, followed by a savage yell, and then another shot, a low groan, and then all was still.

The reader will be at no loss to conjecture who the parties were who were hidden among the broom bushes, from the conversation between Knockdaw and M'Cord in the morning; but as he may not be aware of the cause of such an unexpected occurrence we will hasten to inform him.

Knockdaw and his servant had arrived at the 'Grey Stones of Garlaffin' long before Colville and his party, and to beguile the time, which hung rather heavily on their hand, they applied themselves frequently to a brandy bottle which they had brought with them. After waiting and wearying till night, they had the satisfaction of seeing the parties approach

I

the spot where they were concealed. 'Now, M'Cord, take your pistol in your hand and creep cautiously after me through the bushes. When I halt, I warn you to do the same, for it will be within a few yards of our friends; be sure and bring down Colville, and I'll square accounts with the Captain of the "Speedwell." Now, follow me.' Like serpents they crept along through the rank broom, Knockdaw leading, and M'Cord following close on his trail. While advancing cautiously in this order, the projecting twig of a bush caught the trigger of M'Cord's pistol, and the next moment the contents of it were lodged in Knockdaw's body. In the twinkling of an eye it flashed across the Laird's mind that M'Cord had betrayed him, and turning suddenly round, with a horrid imprecation, he shot M'Cord dead on the spot.

'Follow me!' shouted Captain Girvan, as he dashed into the thicket; but before he proceeded many yards he found Knockdaw and M'Cord lying together in the cold embrace of death.

'They have saved the country a considerable amount of annoyance and cash,' observed Mr Colville, when he recognized who they were.

'What is to be done with the bodies?' asked Jack M'Creadie. 'You see, gentlemen, it's a great advantage to die at sea. There you're sure to get a cool, clean resting-place, and there's no undertaker's fees to pay.'

'It's a sad end to come to,' observed Captain Girvan.

'Ramsey, you'll better go and bring a machine from the inn, and recollect, don't say a word about this to any one. We'll remove the bodies to Knockdaw immediately.'

Accordingly that night the corpses of Knockdaw and his worthless servant were conveyed home, but, secretly as it was done, the truth became known shortly afterwards; and when Mary Ferguson was declared to be Katherine Kennedy, and the heiress of Bennane, Peggy M'Hatteric was heard exclaiming for two-three days—'I aye tauld ye Mary Ferguson wad turn oot tae be a graud leddy yet.'

Mary was more astonished than pleased at her good fortune. With her kind foster parents she was quite happy—a boon neither rank nor riches can confer.

Jack M'Creadie, shortly after these exciting events, was duly wed to Miss Maclure, and Katie, for a few years successively, presented Jack with a son. Many of their descendants are yet about Ballantrae.

Bryce Girvan, the intrepid captain of the 'Speedwell,' left the port of Ballantrae in the evening, a few days after the tragic occurrence at the 'Grey Stones of Garlaffin,' and never to this day has his fate been learned. There was a stiff breeze of south-west wind, and it is supposed that, in his anxiety to make a quick run and return to his first and only love, he crowded on too much sail, and went down in the bay. Be this as it may, not a spar belonging to the 'Speedwell' was ever washed ashore.

The heiress of Bennane mourned his loss for many a day, but time, the great alleviator of human woe, reconciled her to her fate; and after the lapse of a few years she wed a distant relation, and lived to see her grandchildren gather ferns among the GREY STONES OF GARLAFFIN.

CRUGGLETON CASTLE.

A TALE OF GALLOWAY.

CHAPTER I.

A SHORT distance from the Royal Burgh of Whithorn, on the coast, stands the ruins of Cruggleton Castle. Nothing now remains of that vast feudal fortress except a ruined archway, which looks as if it would topple over into the sea at no distant date. The spot on which the castle stood is a kind of promontory, formed by a small bay on each side, and elevated about two hundred feet above the level of the sea, which moans and fumes, like the departed spirits of its lords, around the base of the rock on which it was built. The fosse in front of it, which was the only accessible part of the castle, encloses upwards of an acre of ground, and is still quite visible. Those who are fond of the grand and picturesque would do well to visit this hoary ruin. A pleasant drive of half-an-hour or so takes the denizen of the overcrowded town or city from Whithorn to this sweet secluded spot; at least *Charlie*, a diminutive pony from Shetland or Orkney, we forget which, conveyed the writer of this tradition in about that time.

Cruggleton Castle had long defied all the power of the minions of England to take it. The Laird, Willie Ker, was young, intrepid, and fearless, and looked down, like an eagle from its eyre, with haughty contempt upon the efforts of Comyn to wrest it from him. It was after repulsing his assailants with great slaughter, that the Laird of Castle Feather and Ker sat together, in a spacious room overlooking the sea, in earnest conversation.

'I tell thee, Ker, thou'rt too careless about thy castle,' said Douglas, in a warning voice; ' I have heard it said that Lord Soulis, to whom thou'rt going to accord welcome to-morrow, is a secret partizan of the English—therefore I pray thee to beware.'

Ker laughed gaily ere he replied. 'Know'st thou not, Douglas, that Lord Soulis was one of my father's firmest friends, and think'st thou he would enter my castle as a friend to betray it into the hands of the English. I could not harbour such a base opinion of any man.'

'Always the way with the young and inexperienced. They judge the world by their own unsophisticated heart, until they receive a severe lesson, which Heaven forbid you should ever do; for, if any ill would befall thee, Mary would assuredly break her heart.'

'I know thy tongue is guileless and thy heart true; therefore, I thank thee for thy friendly advice. Rest assured I will neglect no necessary precaution.'

'Have you not a retainer of Lord Soulis in the castle just now?'

'Yes, yes, but he brought the message of his Lordship's coming, and my henchman, Gordon, says he goes moping about the castle like an owl. It seems he's in great sorrow about a brother of his who was lately slain.'

'Where, or by whom?'

'What a question, Douglas! Dost thou think I would ask?'

'Thou should'st, and if his answer was not satisfactory I would turn him out of the castle. Perhaps he's taking a plan of the fortress when he's going moping about, and it's just possible that the tale about his brother's death is all a myth.'

'Take a glass of wine, Douglas, and dispel these idle suspicions. What do I regard either Lord Soulis or his servant?'

'I'll drink no wine to-night, Ker,' said the old Laird of Castle Feather, rising and preparing to leave. 'Be on thy guard, Willie, for I have a presentiment on my mind that some dreadful calamity is about to befall thee.'

The very earnestness of the Douglas had a depressing effect on the mind of Ker, therefore he remained silent as he followed his visitor to the gate of the castle, where his horse was waiting.

Mounting his steed his keen grey eyes rested on the face of Lord Soulis' retainer, who was so intently looking at the fosse in front of the castle that he observed them not.

'Is that the melancholy chiel we were speaking about?' asked the old Laird in a low voice.

'The same.'

'Then by St Ninian I would hurl him over the parapet into the sea; he's an ill-looking thief, and if he's not drowned he'll be hung.' As the Laird said this he rode off, leaving Ker to his meditations.

While the foregoing conversation was taking place between the Laird of Cruggleten and Douglas, Comyn, one of the aspirants for the Scottish crown, and Lord Soulis, a blood relation of his, were sitting *tete-a-tete* in the Priory of Whithorn. The Prior, more through fear than love, professed to be friendly to the English cause; therefore his gates were open to Comyn, who was known to be a creature of Edward's, the English king.

'So you have got Bertram introduced into Cruggleton,' observed Comyn to Lord Soulis.

'Yes, and rest assured he will scan the castle with a critical eye. Would to God I had a thousand followers like him. I could subdue Scotland.'

'The robber Wallace is likely to subdue us, if more energetic measures are not adopted for his suppression,' said Comyn, dryly.

'Never mind Wallace at present, it's Percy's business to look after him; let us endeavour to sup in Cruggleton to-morrow night.'

'I would rather than all the gold in Whithorn; but how is it to be accomplished? I have lost some hundreds of good men already trying to gain admittance, and I'm on the wrong side of it yet.'

'You mean the outside. Well, leave it to me and Bertram, and we'll see what can be done.'

'Will you require many men?'

'No, no; whatever is accomplished will depend more on cunning than force; but remember I will expect a coronet when you are raised to the Scottish throne.'

'You will have earned one. Let us drink success to your enterprise.'

They filled their goblets with the sparkling wine belonging to the Priory, and sat long discussing their treacherous plot. At length, having nearly exhausted their flagons and their theme of discourse—the capture of Cruggleton—they retired for the night.

By noon on the following day Lord Soulis and a few of his trusty followers arrived at the castle, where they were made right welcome. Dinner was served up in the great banqueting hall, and wine, sentiment, and song, circulated freely. Lord Soulis completely threw his inexperienced host off his guard by his warm eulogiums of Wallace. He perceived in a moment that the young enthusiastic Laird of Cruggleton entered heart and soul into the daring exploits of the champion of his enslaved country; and when he saw his eyes dilate as he leaned forward least a word of the exciting theme should escape him, he felt assured he had touched the chord that vibrated to his heart. Having secured the entire confidence of the Laird, Lord Soulis left the table as soon as possible, and, under pretext of enjoying a solitary half-hour, sought the battlements.

The afternoon was beautiful, scarcely a breath of wind ruffled the surface of the sleeping sea. But what cared the perfidious Soulis for the wild grandeur of the rugged coast, the song of birds, or the fragrance of flowers! His mind was busy devising a scheme for betraying not only the castle, but its young, confiding Laird, into the hands of his bitterest enemies, and, Judas-like, he meant to accomplish his ruin with the kiss of friendship.

He sat down on the parapet, where he considered he would be least observed, and gazed anxiously around him. In a moment he was joined by Bertram.

'Sit here beside me, Bertram,' said his Lordship, in a scarcely audible voice. 'Well, have you made a survey of this falcon's eyre?'

'I have.'

'And what is your opinion?'

'It's impregnable,' replied Bertram, who was evidently a man of few words.

'You mean it's impossible to force an entrance.'

'Exactly.'

'But is it not possible to gain admittance by the gate by a little artifice?'

'That entirely depends on the vigilance of the sentinels. Recollect every precaution is taken here the same as in a regular garrison.'

' Well, well, the sentries must be thrown into the moat at the moment I leave the hall and drop a lighted torch from the battlements. This is the signal agreed on between Comyn and me. He will leave Whithorn with two hundred men by nightfall. Remember your life depends on your bravery and intrepidity.'

' More lives than mine depend, say rather, on our treachery,' muttered Bertram, as he looked after his Lordship descending from the battlements.

Never had the Laird of Cruggleton spent a more pleasant afternoon than in the company of the brilliant Lord Soulis. Sitting at the supper table he was quite delighted with the frank, manly manner in which Soulis spoke of the wrongs of Scotland. How ungracious, he thought it was, of the Laird of Castle Feather to be so suspicious of such a noble, fearless advocate of Scotland's rights as Lord Soulis; but he would read him a fine lecture on his want of faith the first time they met. In the meantime, Soulis pressed the wine on his young host, calling on him to pledge him to the success of this project and that for freeing Scotland from English misrule and oppression. At last Soulis rose from the table and begged to be excused for a moment, as he had neglected to give his henchman some important instructions. He might have been absent about ten minutes, when a retainer rushed into the hall with his sword dripping, exclaiming—' Fly, Laird, we are betrayed !' As he cried this, he staggered and fell lifeless at his master's feet.

The clanging of swords, and the yells of men engaged in deadly conflict, now struck upon the Laird's ears. Starting up instinctively he rushed to the hall door, but here he was met by an overwhelming force of Soulis' followers, headed by the treacherous Bertram, who cried exultantly—' Now yield thee, Ker, for escape is impossible.'

' Never to a perfidious craven like thee !' exclaimed Ker, as he sprang suddenly forward and passed his sword through his body, exclaiming as he did so, ' That's for thy treachery, base born hound.'

' On him, my brave men ! cut him down where he stands,' cried a voice in the rear that he instantly recognized as that of Lord Soulis. Pressed on every side, Ker retreated, parrying the blows as well as he could, until he reached the extremity of the hall, when, quick as lightning, he sprang into a room enveloped in total darkness. His cowardly assailants rushed in after him, thinking they now had him securely in their toils, but in this they were doomed to disappointment.

CHAPTER II.

LORD SOULIS ordered lights to be brought, thinking that his men had only to lay their hands on the Laird crouched up in some corner of the room, but to their great astonishment, when lights were procured, they found it empty; and, what added to the disappointment of his Lordship, there seemed no way of exit but by the door through which they had entered.

'There must be some mystery here, my brave followers,' observed his Lordship, looking round on their terror-stricken faces, for it was a superstitious age, and the man who was fearless and brave in battle or foray trembled to face the Powers of Darkness.

'Are you sure he entered the room, my Lord?' asked a young aspirant for knighthood.

'Yes, yes,' cried Soulis, impatiently. 'Strike the panelling with the hilt of your swords; there must be some secret passage leading from the room.'

The men obeyed, and sounded the oaken wainscoting until his Lordship ordered them to desist. The idea that the Laird of Cruggleton might that moment be within a few yards of him made Soulis feel anything but comfortable, after the base, treacherous part he had acted, and it was with some reluctance he left the room and ordered his followers to form a cordon round the castle, so as to prevent his escape.

'The man who brings me the body of Ker, dead or alive, shall be handsomely rewarded,' exclaimed his Lordship, as he saw his retainers depart to execute his commands.

The room, into which the young Laird had so suddenly sprung, had been planned for an emergency like the present. By touching a secret spring in one of the panels, well known to Ker, an entrance was opened displaying a flight of rough steps leading to the base of the rock on which the castle was built. Descending these hurriedly, he reached the sea level. Clambering over the huge boulders, he commenced to

ascend the precipitous boundary of the small bay to the north
of the castle. Having accomplished this task, he halted a
moment to recover his breath, and consider what was the best
course to pursue. If he took the road to Whithorn his enemies
might overtake him, and he shrewdly guessed his fate if he
fell into their hands. Again, if he sought refuge in Castle
Feather, he might involve his friend in his own fate. His
followers, he was sure, would be put to the sword, and how to
act or what to do he knew not. Casting a fond look at his
paternal castle, he dashed a tear from his eye, and muttering,
' There will be a day of terrible reckoning for this yet, my Lord
Soulis,' took his way along the rugged coast.

Strongly as Cruggleton was fortified by nature, the castle
of Douglas seemed to outrival it. Around the base of the rock
on which it was perched, the sea seems never to be at rest;
and the ocean, as it rushes through fissures and caves in the
rocks around it, formed we suppose by the lapse of time and
the strong tides which run along the coast, has a wild, weird
sound which strikes a chill to the heart. Having at length
reached in safety this point, the Laird of Cruggleton sat down
and gazed wistfully at the strong feudal fortress of his truest
friend, and the abode of the peerless Mary—his only daughter
—who had sported with him along the rocky beach from her
infancy. He loved her fondly and truly, and her father both
knew and approved of Mary's choice.

' But what will she think of me now ? ' sighed Willie Ker,
as he seated himself on a fragment of rock and gazed down on
the restless waves. It was just getting lighter in the east
when gradually he fell into a calm sleep, induced, no doubt, by
a night of anxiety and toil. How long he had slept he knew
not, when he was aroused from his slumber by the clashing of
swords and the fierce imprecations of men in deadly conflict,
but scarcely had his eyes rested on the combatants a moment,
when he saw the most powerful of the two force the other over
the precipitous rock into the dread abyss below. Laying down
his sword, he wiped the perspiration from his brow, and turning round to where Ker was standing, he said, ' That was a
tough job, Laird.'

' Gordon !' exclaimed the Laird, ' I never thought to see
you again. My brave henchman, how did you make your
escape ? '

' By preferring the water of the moat to Lord Soulis' mercy.'

' But how did you find your way here ? '

' Oh ! I thought Douglas would like to hear the news from me as well as a stranger, and I wanted to break your misfortune as gently to bonnie Mary as possible.'

' Gordon, I trust in God I'll have it in my power to reward thee yet ; but tell me who he was whom I saw thee hurl over the rock ? '

' No friend of thine, I can assure thee. When I came up he was in the act of sending thee to sleep for ever, but you see he dug a pit and fell into it himself.'

. ' And a fearful pit it is,' said Ker, shuddering, as he peered over the ledge of the rock.

' He'll never return to the cowardly Soulis to tell him tales, I'll swear.'

' What are we going to do, Gordon ? '

' Let us have some breakfast with your old, tried friend, Douglas, and we'll hear what he advises.'

This suggestion of Gordon's was quite agreeably received by the Laird, so they hastened round to the gate and demanded admittance.

It is impossible to describe the indignation of the Laird of Castle Feather when he heard the tale of bloodshed and wrong.

' My unfortunate dear friend, such deeds dare not have been committed during the wise reign of Alexander, but there's no redress now for such a foul dastardly deed but one, and I doubt it would be unsuccessful. However, we'll see, we'll see,' said Douglas, in a musing tone. ' In the meantime, we must have breakfast.'

Although advanced in years, the Laird of Castle Feather was still active and hale, and during the morning meal he was busy forming plans and rejecting them. He never once said to the young Laird, 'If you had taken my advice and warning this calamity would have been averted.' He rather admired Ker for his unsuspicious nature, well knowing it was the index of a noble, generous disposition. As soon as breakfast was over, he said to Mary—' You may retire, dear ; we are going to hold a council of war.' Mary bowed and withdrew, and with the tears streaming down her girlish face, for to her inexperienced mind the whole seemed so strange, unaccountable, and savage, that she thought it all a hideous dream.

'Now,' said Douglas, breaking silence, when the door shut, 'there's but one course you can pursue; summon your vassals here, and I'll gather mine together as soon as I consider it prudent, and with caution and cunning we may regain the castle.'

'This is my quarrel, Douglas, and sorry would I be to drag thee into it.'

'It's every honest man's quarrel, sir, who has the least sense of justice or honour left in him. If this hellish work is to go unpunished, let us assume the distaff or the cowl, and, like the monks, sing of peace and rest in heaven, for we'll get none in Scotland.'

'That's my opinion, Laird,' observed Gordon, who was perfectly delighted with the fire displayed by Douglas.

'It's also my opinion, but I know the castle is impregnable if properly guarded, and I feel to bring ruin on my best and truest friend.'

'Will you leave Soulis in possession, or are you determined to endeavour to regain Cruggleton?'

'That will be my determination, until I either sleep in it or the grave. Think'st thou, dear Douglas, I can ever forget or forgive last night's outrage and wrong?'

'I think not, else thou'rt unworthy of thy noble sire or Mary's hand. Seek thou the maiden and comfort her: Gordon, come with me.'

Leaving Ker and Douglas to mature their plans, let us return to Cruggleton.

At an early hour Lord Soulis left the castle, and rode direct across the waste moorland, which then separated it from Whithorn, attended by a few of his followers, for he feared to trust himself alone through a district where he knew Ker had many friends. All impatient to communicate the news of the capture of the castle, he rode rapidly up the wide street of the village, closely followed by his retainers, and halted at the principal entrance to the Priory, and was immediately shown by a sleek brother of the fraternity to the suite of apartments set apart for Comyn's use.

'I doubt you are too early astir, my Lord, to bring good tidings,' observed Comyn, smiling, and extending his hand to his friend.

'Cruggleton is yours, when you choose to occupy it, my Lord.'

' Impossible! Soulis, this shall not be forgotten. How did you accomplish it? Did you lose many men? Have you slain or captured Ker?'

' Neither.'

' Ha! did he escape?'

' Yes.'

' That's unfortunate. He may trouble us again.'

' It must be alone, then, for the greater part of his followers are laid out for burial in the courtyard.'

' Good! Just sit down a minute until I dress, and I'll ride over and see this renowned castle. I think, Soulis, this should raise me in the estimation of Edward.'

' No doubt of it, my Lord. The craven Lord of Galloway, John Baliol, I'm told, is rapidly sinking in the estimation of Edward.'

' He's too obsequious, time-serving, and spiritless to rule Scotland at any rate.'

Of course the ambitious Soulis acquiesced in the sentiments of the haughty aspirant for the crown, although he well knew they had been guilty of as mean and dastardly an action as ever had been perpetrated by the sycophant Baliol, in the base, treacherous manner they had become possessed of Cruggleton.

As soon as Comyn had dressed, and summoned his numerous followers, they bade good-bye to the worthy Prior, and started for the castle. As they rode over the moor, Soulis briefly related the night's adventure to Comyn, as he termed it, remarking, however, that Ker had slain his accomplished henchman Bertram, and as yet he was uncertain of the fate of Foster, whom he had sent along the coast in quest of Ker.

' What a noble castle!' exclaimed Comyn, upon entering the court. ' I could defend it with a hundred men against the power of England.'

' It's yours, noble Comyn; and long may you live to enjoy the lordly pile.'

' Thanks, Soulis, many thanks. Now, since I'm master here, let us dedicate this evening to hilarity; there's little danger to apprehend from Ker for a long time to come.'

In regal state Comyn sat that evening at the head of the table, while Soulis occupied the seat of honour on his right; on the left were a few knights and their ladies, who looked up admiringly at the great Comyn, who was destined, they hoped, at no distant day to rule Scotland. After dinner was served, and the wine set on the table, the minstrels were ordered in, and mirth and music resounded through the great hall at Cruggleton.

'Among other trophies won from Ker last night, we managed to capture his favourite minstrel,' observed Soulis, laughing and filling his silver goblet with wine.

'Let him be sent for immediately, I wish to hear him sing.'

Accordingly one of the pages was despatched for Grey, and in the course of a few minutes he returned with an old man bearing a harp, Grey had entered the service of the late Laird of Cruggleton when a boy, therefore he was deeply attached to the young Laird. It may be imagined he was in no mood for singing, but knowing he imperilled his life by refusing, he ran his fingers rapidly over the harp, and sung—

'Cruggleton, beneath thy archway,
  Leaning o'er the restless sea,
Have I sat beside a maiden
  Fairer, dearer far to me
Than the azure of the ocean ;
  Than the fragrant clover lea ;
Than ambition, fame, or glory,
  Or ancestral pedigree !'

'My Lord Soulis,' shouted a retainer, rushing into the hall, in breathless haste, 'the castle is attacked on all sides by Ker !'

CHAPTER III.

In a moment's time the mirth was hushed, and the merry laugh and ready jest were succeeded by the screaming of ladies, as they rushed pell-mell from the lighted hall to seek a place of safety. All was alarm and consternation, and Lord Soulis and Comyn were terror-stricken, for well they knew what their fate would be if they fell into the hands of the deeply-wronged Laird. Not a moment, however, was to be lost, so drawing their swords they ran to the battlements, crying on their retainers to follow them.

Meantime the battle at the drawbridge was fierce and furious. Ker and Gordon had swam the moat with about a score of the bravest men, and had managed to reach the bridge unseen, but in the act of lowering it the armed retainers of Soulis caught the alarm and rushed to the rescue of the sentinels in over-powering numbers. Seeing the bridge unlowered, and hearing the battle raging inside, the old Laird of Castle Feather ordered his men to cross the moat and assist Ker. Soulis and Comyn now reached the point so bravely contested, and encouraged their men by word and action. Ker saw his men, as they came up in the darkness and confusion, stricken down, until only Gordon remained fighting at his side. By this time they were forced back to the verge of the fosse, and perceiving that all was lost, Gordon shouted, ' Follow me,' and sprang into the water. Ker hesitated a moment and then followed his dauntless henchman.

'Lower the bridge, my gallant men, and pursue Ker,' shouted Soulis at the top of his voice. ' If he escapes, never return to me.'

Douglas waited until he heard this order given, and knowing that all was lost, he mounted his steed and rode rapidly home to guard his own castle. After what he had witnessed, he mentally resolved that his enemies would not find him napping at his post.

The night was dark and stormy as Ker and Gordon fled across the moor in the direction of Whithorn. Sometimes they could hear the cries of their pursuers, but being on foot they managed to elude them, and before day reached Whithorn, wet, dejected, and completely worn out.

' I wonder what pretty Susan will think of her gallant lover this morning,' said Gordon, trying to assume a gaiety he did not feel.

'To whom do you allude ? ' asked Ker, in a dejected tone.

'To my sweetheart, Laird, and this is where she lives,' answered Gordon, as he tapped at the door of a very humble, low-thatched cottage.

' Who's there ? ' asked a sweet feminine voice.

' For the love of our blessed Lady, Susan, open the door. Here is the young Laird of Cruggleton quite impatient to see your flaxen curls and laughing blue eyes.'

' Stay a minute, and I'll admit ye,' for she had by this time heard of the taking of Cruggleton, and, thinking her lover had been slain, she did not take long to dress.

The door was unbarred, and Ker and Gordon entered, but in the dark entry Susan mistook Ker for her lover, and, as he was foremost, she wound her arms around his neck and gave him a kiss of welcome.

'I doubt you have made a mistake, Susan; but no matter, I'll get two at your earliest convenience.'

'Come this way,' said Susan; 'how wet and cold you are. Off with your clothes, both of ye, I'll bring you a change of my father's.' As she said this she hurried them into a small bedroom, lighted a fire, brought them dry raiment, set bread, milk, and cheese, on the table, told them to make themselves as comfortable as they could, and then retired. They made a hearty meal, and, feeling sorely fatigued, they threw themselves on the bed and slept until the morning was far advanced.

Susan, knowing the danger her lover was in, slept little, and at an early hour she was out through the village, gleaning all the news.

'You are closely pursued,' observed Susan, as she set breakfast before the fugitives; 'Comyn's men have been ranging the village all morning. But I have also heard good news.'

'What is it?' exclaimed the young men, in one voice.

'Wallace has defeated the English, with great slaughter, at a place in Ayrshire called Loudon Hill, and has marched into Galloway to retake the castles held by the Southroners.'

'That is indeed good news, Susan, but I doubt it's too good to be true,' observed Ker, in a musing tone of voice.

'I'm led to believe it's true,' persisted Susan, 'for I heard Friar Logan say to Laird Garlies that Wallace's army was encamped at Minigaff, and that's not far from this.'

'Thank God,' exclaimed Ker, fervently; 'this has infused new life into me. If it was dark I would join his standard before sunrise.'

'And I'll accompany thee,' cried Gordon, enthusiastically.

'Oh, Jamie, what a resolution,' exclaimed Susan, wringing her hands and looking piteously in his face.

'Oh, Susan,' exclaimed Gordon, in the same tone as his sweetheart, 'would'st thou like to see me going skulking about the village, when brave men were pouring out their blood like water to free our country from the yoke of Edward.'

'I would not,' answered Susan, stoutly, drying her eyes.

'There's the kiss I promised thee last night. Thou'rt a brave lass.'

Everything being arranged for the departure of the fugitives, at nightfall they took their departure, but not until the Laird of Cruggleton had given Susan instructions to go to Castle Feather and acquaint Mary Douglas of his determination to join Wallace, and of his unalterable love. 'Say to her aged father that I hope to return before long, and yet wrest my castle from the base miscreant, Soulis, and his hired assassins.' This mission Susan promised faithfully to fulfil, and with many tears she bade them God speed.

Wishing to avoid Wigtown, the fugitives left the road and struck across the fields; but not being perfectly acquainted with the locality, they lost their way, and a considerable portion of time trying to find it. As soon as their pursuers observed this they redoubled their speed, kept on right through Wigtown, and, at the base of the hill on which the town is built, lay in ambush.

Along the hill side came the fugitives, congratulating themselves that their enemies had given up the pursuit, when suddenly a dozen of stalwart ruffians sprang on the road before them, and cried—'Now yield thee, Ker, Lord Soulis and Comyn lack thy company.'

'Never, while I can wield this good sword!' exclaimed Ker, striking the leader and spokesman to the earth. This was the signal for a general onslaught. With yells and execrations the whole band rushed forward, but scarcely had they done so when from the wood, on the opposite side of the road, there rushed forth about fifty men, headed by Wallace.

'Down with Comyn's base serfs!' shouted Wallace, in that clear commanding voice that could ever be heard above the roar of battle, as he rushed into the thickest of the *melee.* 'Spare them not,' he cried, as at each sweep of his tremendous sword he laid another on the road.

In less time than we have taken to narrate it, the followers of Soulis and Comyn were all slain but one, who acted on the maxim—'He that fights, and runs away, may live to fight another day.' This craven fled into Wigtown, alarmed the castle, told the Governor that Wallace was advancing at the head of a victorious army, and that he had alone escaped to tell the news. The Governor was a very prudent gentleman, who regarded the Scot, but specially Wallace, as a thorough-bred savage, and having heard of the defeat of his countrymen, in a regular battle, he evacuated the castle at once, and in such haste were they to depart that all the valuable stores it contained fell into Wallace's hands, without striking a blow.

Having thus obtained possession of the castle, Wallace appointed Adam Gordon, the ancestor of the noble house of Kenmuir, to the Governorship of the castle, and then calling a council of gentlemen, who had joined his standard, he ordered the Laird of Cruggleton to state his grievance, and how he had earned the hatred of Comyn.

He commenced and briefly related, in a modest style, all the incidents with which the reader is already acquainted, and ended by saying—'The liberty of my country has been ever dearer to me than life, and if you are pleased, sir, to accept of my humble services, I shall never disgrace the noble cause in which you are embarked.'

'And have you an ambition to re-take your castle from the detestable wretch who holds it?' asked Sir William Douglas, the Laird of Douglasdale, and head of a great family.

'That is my ambition, but I am powerless to do so. In trying to re-take it, all my followers were slain, with the exception of one, and he is here.'

'It's most fortunate for you, Laird, that I was intending to surprise this castle last night,' observed Wallace, as he gazed admiringly at the noble bearing, and handsome, frank face of Ker.

'Had it not been for your timely interference I would have been overpowered and slain, for I never would have yielded to the serfs of Comyn and Soulis.'

'What have you got to say, Sir James Graham, to this affair? Can you suggest nothing?'

'My unfortunate country has certainly sunk very low, when such deeds can be perpetrated openly. To think that an aspirant to the throne of Scotland would disgrace himself so is beyond my comprehension, and gives me a low idea of our nobles indeed.'

'You tell me, Ker, your castle is strong. I believe your statement; I have heard favourable mention of it before; but strong as it is, I will assist you to retake it, if you faithfully promise, on the word of a true knight, never to desert your country's cause.'

'I swear before the gentlemen here assembled that while a

southern foe pollutes the soil of Scotland, I will never let my good sword rest.'

'Enough. Now you may retire, and to-morrow evening you will act as guide to Cruggleton.'

When Ker descended the stair and told Gordon the result of his enterprise, he danced, shouted, and cut the most fantastic capers through the room, singing as he did so—

> Cruggleton, within thy bowers,
> I may love my lass again.

CHAPTER IV.

AFTER Ker's defeat, Lord Soulis and Comyn held an earnest conference. Had he been slain or captured, their minds would have been at rest, but with such an active, brave, determined foe alive, they could not but be uneasy and alarmed. Men were ordered to every assailable point of the castle, and the man who neglected his duty was promised a short shrive and a long rope.

The space around the drawbridge was literally strewn with the bodies of retainers belonging to Ker, Soulis, and Comyn, and, witnessed in the dawn of day, presented a ghastly scene. No one thought of retiring to rest, and as Comyn was not renowned for being extra brave, he resolved to leave the castle as quickly as possible, and leave Soulis in possession in the meantime. The very fact of Ker disappearing so mysteriously on the night that Lord Soulis attacked it made him arrive at this conclusion at once. He naturally reasoned that if he knew a secret way out, he was sure to know the road back again, and possibly he might strike a dagger to his heart when he was sleeping.

After breakfast the ladies declared they would not stay another night in such a castle for the wealth of a kingdom; and as they could not travel alone, their knights had a good excuse for leaving also. Soulis was no way annoyed by this, but he could scarcely suppress his ire when Comyn announced his departure for Dumfries.

'Will you take your retainers with you, my lord?' asked Soulis as calmly as he could.

'I cannot well travel without them, but I'll leave you a few.'

'I need them not. If this castle is properly guarded a dozen of men could defend it against a thousand,' said Soulis, proudly.

'I'm perfectly aware of that, else I would not leave. I should know something of its capabilities, seeing the men and money it has cost me.'

'And never took it,' sneered Soulis.

'That task was reserved for a man with more cunning than—'

'Bravery,' said Soulis, smiling. 'But it would be very impolitic of us to quarrel, therefore we will let the subject rest.'

'You are right, Soulis. There's my hand.'

'You will find all right upon your return,' said Soulis, taking his proffered hand and shaking it warmly. He did this not through love but policy. He liked him as well, however, as villains generally do each other.

Soulis stood by the drawbridge until Comyn and the greater part of his retainers passed; then waving his adieu, he returned to the castle, mentally resolving to retain it for his own use, seeing he had risked so much to obtain possession.

Comyn rode across the waste moor, in the direction of Whithorn, heartily congratulating himself of being clear of such unsafe quarters; but upon reaching the Priory, great was his astonishment to learn that Wallace was in Wigtown, and that the English governor of the castle had fled. Now he deeply regretted leaving Cruggleton, but to return and tell Soulis that he was afraid to encounter Wallace was to proclaim himself a coward, therefore he resolved to remain under the holy protection of Prior Scott.

Leaving a sufficient number of men to defend the Castle of Wigtown, Wallace selected a hundred of his bravest men and started for Cruggleton, Ker acting as guide. Passing through Kirkinner, they kept Garliestown on the left and Whithorn on the right, thus adopting a route about equi-distant from both places, their intention being to proceed as secretly as possible to the castle.

The night was calm and beautiful, and the moonbeams danced with a silvery radiance upon the placid sea when Wallace arrived in the vicinity of Cruggleton. Leaving his men a little to the north of the castle, he took with him Ker, Steven, and Gordon—the latter protesting against being left behind—and went forth to reconnoitre. After descending the precipitous rocky boundary of the bay, Wallace declared there was but one way of taking the castle, and that was by scaling the rock on which it was built.

' There are never any sentinels posted on the sea side of the castle, I suppose, Ker?' said Wallace, as he seated himself on a rock and surveyed the dim outlines of the castle.

' You're right in your conjecture, sir ; the west side of the rock is considered impregnable, no living thing, save a sea-bird, has been ever known to ascend the rock.'

' I will ascend it to-night, and if you have not a steady hand and a firm nerve, I advise you not to try it. I know Steven can follow me wherever I go.'

' I have both went up and down many times, when I wanted to see a friend of mine who resides in Whithorn, and did not care about asking permission,' observed Gordon, modestly.

' You're just about the age when one would risk their neck to see a pretty girl, and to-night you shall have the honour of leading the forlorn hope.'

' Many thanks, sir ; believe me, I'm as proud as if I was to be knighted.'

' Perhaps you may earn that honour yet on some well fought field.'

' I know a secret way into the castle, but it would lead us into the hall,' observed Ker.

' The very place I do not want to go just now. We will ascend the rock, with Gordon as a guide. When up, creep stealthily along after the example I will set you. Not a word is to be spoken by any one, no matter what may be the danger or difficulty ; when you come to a sentry, hurl him over the rock into the sea, until we reach the bridge over the fosse. Douglas will lead my men instantly forward when I sound my bugle. These are my final instructions. Gordon, lead the way.'

Having arrived in safety at the bottom of the rock, Gordon looked about him carefully, and, laying hold of a projecting piece of rock, he planted his foot firmly and began his perilous ascent, closely followed by his companions. Slowly, painfully they crept up the sheer precipice, until Gordon was safely up, then bending over the dizzy height, he assisted the others unto the rocky pinnacle beside him.

While the adventurers are drawing their breath, and

preparing for rushing like falcons on their prey, let us hurriedly
glance inside at Lord Soulis and his retainers.

It was a little past midnight, and deep silence pervaded the
castle. About eleven o'clock Soulis had went the rounds of
the sentries, and saw that every man was at the post assigned
him; not that he was afraid of an attack, but it was a military
age and men prided themselves upon their discipline and war-
like attainments. He retired to rest, and by slow degrees he
fell asleep.

There is a kind of sleep that steals upon us sometimes, which,
while it holds the body captive, does not free the mind from a
sense of things about it, and enable it to ramble at its pleasure.
So far as an overpowering drowsiness, a prostration of strength,
and an entire inability to control our thoughts or power of
motion can be called sleep, this is it; and yet we have a
consciousness of everything about us.

Soulis knew perfectly well he was in his room, that his
sword was on the table, and yet he was asleep. Suddenly the
scene changed; there was a suffocating sensation came over
him, and he thought with a glow of terror that he heard a
trumpet sound, mingled with savage cries and the rushing of
many men into his chamber, and he awoke trembling.

'Good heaven, what was that which struck me dumb with
terror!'

From every quarter of the castle came the cry of despair,
the yells of men in a death and life struggle, and the loud
clashing of arms.

Springing out of bed he seized his sword and rushed into
the hall. But is impossible to describe his terror and consternation when, in place of meeting his followers, he was confronted
by Ker and Wallace.

'At last we meet on equal terms, Lord Soulis,' exclaimed
Ker, rushing towards him.

'Oh! spare my life for the sake of former friendship,' cried
Soulis, in despairing accents.

'Such mercy as ye showed my brave followers ye shall receive.
Seize him, my brave men, and hurl him over the battlements.'

Soulis, driven to bay, made an ineffectual struggle to
resist, but he was overpowered in a moment, dragged from the
hall, and while prayers and execrations alternately trembled on
his lips, he was hurled into eternity. By this time such of

his followers as were not slain were consigned to the dungeons of the castle to await their doom.

On the following morning Comyn sat at breakfast with the worthy Prior, laughing and jesting about Ker's disastrous attempt to retake Cruggleton, when his henchman entered and announced the death of Soulis and Ker's success.

'Impossible!' cried the worthless aspirant for the crown of Scotland, as he sprang to his feet pale and trembling. 'Ker had not the means or men to retake the castle.'

'It is nevertheless true; a few of his retainers effected their escape by springing into the moat, and have reached Whithorn. Wallace, who is in company with Ker, is expected here in a few hours.'

This was enough. In a few minutes Comyn was in the saddle fleeing across the country in the direction of Dumfries. Subsequently he received the punishment due to his treachery from the hands of Bruce and Kirkpatrick.

About noon on the following day the Laird of Castle Feather and his beauteous daughter arrived at Cruggleton, and as the old man listened to the tale of how the castle was taken, tears of joy streamed down his aged face. As the castle contained everything needful for man and beast, and as Wallace's band of patriots stood greatly in need of rest, it was arranged that they should remain a few days in such good quarters and recruit their strength. Before leaving, Mary Douglas became Mrs Ker, and Gordon and Susan followed their example, the latter gentleman being left to defend the castle during his master's absence.

Those acquainted with the history of Wallace know that Ker never deserted his standard, that he faithfully fulfilled the pledge given to the illustrious Champion of Scotland in Wigton Castle, and that after Wallace's base betrayal he attached himself to the cause of Bruce, and rose to eminence in that great King's service.

———

NOTE.—As some of the descendants of the brave Laird of Cruggleton are still residing in Galloway, the author of the tale takes this opportunity of stating that in the History of Galloway, published by Nicholson, Kirkcudbright, the name of the Laird is spelled Kerlie and Ker; we adopted the latter, but have since learned that the former is more correct.

GREENAN CASTLE.

CHAPTER I.

GREENAN CASTLE! how many have sat beside its crumbling walls, listening to the hoarse murmur of the waves as they lashed themselves into foam against its rocky foundations, and mused upon the wizard-working power of time. Here, in ages long ago buried in oblivion, knights and ladies held their revels, whilst minstrels sang the bold exploits of its lords by land and sea: now it is tenantless, roofless, and haunted—not by ghosts, but by wandering winds from the Western Sea. To the inhabitants of Ayr it has ever been a place of favourite resort, as it seems to possess charms alike for rich and poor. To the merchant chained to counter or desk, during the dog-days it has irresistible charms. As he saunters along the sand, gazing at the sun setting in golden glory behind the peaks of Arran, or looking at the rippling waves chasing each other in merry gambols o'er the beach, his soul is lifted above the dross of earth to the source of beauty and joy that surrounds him.

It was a beautiful summer's evening, towards the latter end of June, and about the beginning of the fifteenth century—we wish to be not over particular as to dates—that Richard Kennedy sat alone in his chamber in Greenan Castle, musing, not on war, but on the peerless face of Mabel Bruce, who was the only child of Edward Bruce of Cunningpark, which then stood isolated on an island formed by the Doon.

Dick Kennedy, as he was familiarly called in those uncouth days, when girls had faithers and mithers instead of 'papas and mammas,' as they have now-a-days, had set his heart upon winning the beauteous Mabel, but she had set her heart in array against him—that citadel being already occupied by the manly form and handsome face of David Cochrane of Bridgehouse. As we remarked before, Kennedy had set his heart upon winning the 'Rose o' the Isle,' as Mabel was called by all the gallants of Ayr and Alloway parishes ; but how was he to obtain possession of the coveted prize? True, her father was his tenant, and not over rich ; but he did not like to resort to extremes until they could be no longer avoided. Had he been half as much annoyed by a man as he was by the fairy minx, he would have knocked him on the head at once; but he very much doubted if any insult offered to her father was likely to secure her affections. After sitting and looking at the sleeping sea and fleet of fishers' boats which dotted the bay, with sails flapping idly to-and-fro, as they rose and fell with the crestless waves, Dick arose from his recumbent posture, shook himself like a water dog after a swim, lifted his hat, and sauntered forth to the Castle-yard.

'Did you see Macnairston about, Frazer?' asked Kennedy at his favourite groom.

'I saw him, sir, going in the direction of Doonfoot about half an hour ago.'

Without speaking another word, Kennedy took the direction in which he supposed he would find his trusty henchman, Macnairston. Descending the precipitous path which led to the beach, he sauntered dreamily along the sand until he reached the Doon, where he found his servant sitting beneath an alder, fishing.

'What luck, Macnairston?' exclaimed the Laird of Greenan, as soon as he was within hailing distance of his servant.

'Middling, sir,' answered the servant, rising to his feet, laying his rod on the bank, and turning round. 'The truth is, Laird, the trout are sometimes like the lasses, a little capricious in their moods. They'll sometimes take a worm three or four days old, and at other times refuse the most tempting bait,' As Macnairston said this he looked in the direction of Cuningpark and laughed.

'Thou'rt inclined to be enigmatical this evening, Macnairston. Speak out plainly, man, thou know'st I hate riddles.'

'You see, Laird, that the Bridgehouse boat is lying on our side this evening.'

'Well, sirrah! what of that?'

'Oh! nothing particular. The boat is as often at this side of the Doon as the other,' answered the privileged henchman, as he leisurely wound up his line.

'If thou stand'st there puzzling me any longer, by St John
I'll send thy ugly carcase to keep company with the fish to-
night in the deepest pool in the stream.'

Macnairston looked up into the Laird's face, and shuddered
when he observed the passion with which it was convulsed.

'In plain language then, Laird, you have a rival for the fair
Mabel.'

'Thou'rt surely raving mad or jesting, Macnairston; if the
latter, beware.'

'Seeing's believing, sir.'

'What is he, or where is he to be found?' cried the Laird,
laying his hand instinctively on his sword.

'Be calm, sir, and I'll inform ye of the whole affair.'

'Be calm! ye low-born varlet. How dare ye catechise
me,' cried the Laird, fuming with passion, and pacing rapidly
to-and-fro along the bank like a caged hyæna.

Macnairston, seeing his master taking it so sorely to heart,
gathered up his fishing tackle, ascended the bank, and approached him with a half affrighted look, for well he knew he
had a temper not to be triffled with.

'Speak out, man, ye have nothing to fear. Tell me at
once what you know and what you think.'

'I saw, while sitting here, Davie Cochrane, of Bridgehouse,
sauntering along the bank of the stream, as if he expected
some one to meet him. He did not wait long before Mabel
came tripping along, arrayed in the blue silk kirtle and snood
that you admire so much, and jumping into the boat, she was
beside him in a moment's time.'

'Well, well, Macnairston, in Heaven's name come to the
point at once, or I'll throttle ye where ye stand.'

'If ye don't allow me to tell my tale in my own way, I'll
speak no more.'

Kennedy knew his henchman had a dogged, fearless nature,
and as he was anxious to hear out the story which he had so
unreasonably interrupted, he said in a milder voice, 'Come,
come, Macnairston, I won't interrupt you again, supposing you
to spin a yarn that would reach from here to Ailsa.'

'I would not have known,' resumed Macnairston, 'that
Davie was her lover, but the moment she sprung on to the
bank he wound his arms around her, and kissed her more than
once.'

'Holy Virgin! what an ass I must be not to have perceived this long ago. Davie Cochrane, a smooth-faced, chicken-hearted boy, to come and carry off from me the prize upon which I have set my heart. But I'll be revenged on him before long. Macnairston, which way did they go?'

'Whist, sir; see, yonder they come this way, arm in arm. You'll believe me now.' As Macnairston said this, he pointed in the direction in which the lovers were advancing.

'Let us crouch down here and see this game out,' said the Laird, as he seized Macnairston by the arm and dragged him down beside a tree which screened them from the view of the youthful lovers. Evidently Mabel was happy.. Her merry laugh could be heard ringing through the trees as they approached. Each peal of laughter went like a dagger to the Laird's proud, vindictive heart; but he bit his nether lip until the blood came to suppress his indignation. From his hiding place he could see every movement of his hated rival, but when he saw Cochrane fold her to his heart, and kiss her over and over again, it required all the strength and tact of Macnairston to hold him back. Had Cochrane been aware of his proximity to death he would not have lingered so long on the bank of the Doon watching the retreating form of the fair maiden, to whom he was so deeply and faithfully attached; but Heaven in mercy hides these things from human view.

'I'll dispatch the knave where he stands, Macnairston!' exclaimed Kennedy, savagely. 'Let go your grip, or I'll sheath my dagger in your heart.' But Macnairston knew his humour, and heeded him not until Cochrane and Mable were gone.

'Thank God!' exclaimed Macnairston, wiping the perspiration from his brow, 'he's gone. Had you slain him here, in broad daylight, you might have bidden farewell to Greenan for ever. Take my advice, you can square accounts with him when the sun's in the north, without anyone being the wiser of it.'

'I daresay your right, Macnairston; but you know I have little patience with those who thwart me. But it's settled in my mind that either he or I die, and that before many sunsets.'

'I'm quite agreeable, Laird, to see that he's properly cared for as soon as ye think proper, but it must be done quietly.'

Having arrived at this laudable resolution, they returned to the castle in silence. Whatever were their thoughts, each

kept them to himself.   Dick Kennedy retired early to his
chamber, not to sleep, but to concoct his diabolical scheme of
revenge.   How far he was successful the sequel will show.

CHAPTER II.

BETWEEN the father of Mabel Bruce and Davie Cochrane there
had ever existed a firm friendship.   Scarcely a day passed
without an exchange of civility between the Laird of Bridgehouse and the tenant of Cunningpark.   It was, therefore, with
feelings of delight they beheld the growing attachment between
their respective children—David and Mabel.   Their houses lay
so near each other, and they were so often in company together, that it would have been strange, indeed, if their young
susceptible hearts had not been impressed by the rosy god.
As children they had spent many happy hours on the sandy
beach, between Greenan and Ayr, and, as they advanced in
years, their walks were extended to the sweet sylvan glades
along the Doon and the Ayr, where they often repaired to re-
new their vows of love, and dream of blissful years in the
future.

Unfortunately, Mabel's peerless face and form at last attracted the notice of the Laird of Greenan, who had but
recently returned to Scotland, after an absence of many years.
Where or how he had spent his time none knew but Macnairston ; some said in France, others in Italy ; but these were
only idle conjectures, and but few dared to ask the haughty,
rich Laird of Greenan for an account of his peregrinations.

After the incident of the previous evening, he passed a
restless night, and at breakfast he was silent and dull looking.
Macnairston knew his humour too well to disturb him.   At
last the Laird turned round and abruptly said—' Mac, I have
had a bad night of it.'

' Sorry to hear that, sir,' said the henchman, composedly.

' That's a lie ! you don't care a fig I was at the bottom of
the sea,' exclaimed Kennedy, trying to work himself up to fever
heat.

' Thanks for the compliment, sir.'

' You knew of this cursed love affair long ago, for you are
eternally about the Doon.'

'I did not. I have seen them sometimes together, but I never suspected Cochrane was wooing the damsel.'

'Ha! ha! how innocent you are, Mac; you are the most consummate hypocrite ever I met.'

'I studied under a good master.'

'This to me, you knave! Beware of exciting me this morning.'

'You're exciting yourself, sir. Was I in your position I would win the damsel first, and then woo her at my leisure.'

'Sit down, Mac; I was thinking of that scheme, but how is it to be carried out?'

'It's simple, quite simple, sir.'

'Pray explain yourself.'

'I will endeavour to see Cochrane to-day, and ascertain, if possible, on what night he is going to meet her again; this done, I will set a gin for the pretty bird.'

'Let me hear your plan of trapping her; I don't like any mystery between you and me.'

'Well, if you cannot trust me to work it safely out, I'll tell you all about it. If he is to meet her to-night on the banks of the Doon as usual, I will get a boy that I can depend on to convey a message to the beauteous Mabel, that an unforeseen circumstance has occurred to prevent him keeping his appointment as he has to go immediately to Dunure on his father's business; but that he expects to return about nine o'clock, and that it would give him the greatest pleasure to meet her about Greenan. Of course you'll understand Cochrane will wait for her at the trysting tree, while you convey her safely to the castle.'

'The plan is worthy of your fertile brain; but if we were seen——'

'We will be disguised,' interrupted Mac.

'I am beginning to understand, but what about the boy?'

'You'll never do for a diplomatist—I'll be the boy to Mr Cochrane. But if this scheme does not meet your approbation, I'll tell you of another which might be resorted to, although I would prefer the first.'

'Well, let me hear it.'

'Edward Bruce is your tenant, and not overly burdened with worldly gear.'

'Well, proceed,' said the Laird approvingly, seeing Mac seemed to hesitate.

'I would pay Mr Bruce a visit, tell him your honourable

intentions—that is, if you are really in earnest—show him how comfortable and happy you are capable of making his daughter, and hear what he says to that. If he refuses his consent to your union, then play your last card—threaten *eviction.*'

'You are an invaluable follower, Mac,' ejaculated the Laird, warmly.

'If the proposal which I think you are inclined to make miscarries, I will hear another tale this evening ; and bethink you ere you commit yourself. If your offer is rejected, it will put them on the *qui vive.*'

'I never thought on that, Mac; you are the best at setting up pins and knocking them down ever I met.'

'You know, sir, there are two ways of looking at anything.'

'Get my horse ready, and I'll ride over to Cunningpark and see how the land lies.'

'Will I accompany you ?'

'No.'

'I would have gloried in witnessing his humiliation,' muttered Macnairston, on his way to the stable. 'He thinks because he's rich and powerful, forsooth, that he has only to be obeyed; but he'll meet with a great disappointment this day. I know they're betrothed, and that Edward Bruce will refuse his offer with scorn, for I have led him to detest the proud, heartless Laird of Greenan. He imagines I have forgotten the gross outrage he committed on the only girl ever I loved; but before this game is played out I'll teach the tyrant I have feelings as well as he.' Entering the stable, he ordered Frazer to saddle the Laird's horse, and lead him round to the hall door. Feeling confident Kennedy would meet with a refusal, Macnairston took his way across the fields to Bridge-house to have a chat with the lover of Mabel.

During his ride along the sands from Greenau to Cunningpark, pride and love alternately ruled the heart of the haughty Laird. More than twenty times he reined up his steed on the short way between the two houses, but at last love gained the mastery, and he rode forward at a brisk pace. He found Mr Bruce at home, and after a few preliminary remarks about the weather, he introduced the cause of his visit and his matrimonial intentions by observing that since his return to Scotland to heir the estate he had resolved to take a wife and settle down for life.

'A most laudable resolution, Laird, seeing you are reputed to have the wherewith to maintain one in pomp and splendour. No doubt you have fixed on the damsel that is to be so favoured,' observed Mr Bruce, quietly.

Kennedy cast a sharp, scrutinising look at Mr Bruce's face, but there was nothing in it discouraging or sneering. 'Yes, Mr Bruce, but the young lady that I have set my heart upon may not accept of my offer.'

'That's quite possible. Young ladies have sometimes strange fancies, and often choose men for husbands whom their parents think unsuitable for them.'

'Do you not think, Mr Bruce, that it's the duty of a father to interfere, when by so doing he might insure his daughter's happiness?'

'Ay, if we were sure of securing their happiness it would be right to use a little coercion, but experience teaches us that our opinions and estimates of human character are often erroneous. Therefore I have resolved that my daughter will have the privilege of choosing or refusing as her fancy dictates.'

'It was of Mabel I was going to speak. In a word, Mr Bruce, I am devotedly attached to her. I love her with my whole heart, although I have never spoken to her on the subject.'

There was something so straightforward and honest in this avowal—something so different from Macnairston's representations of Kennedy's character—that Mr Bruce was completely taken by surprise.

'Laird, you astonish me!' exclaimed Bruce. 'Mabel is so unfitted for the exalted position to which you have honourably proposed to raise her, that really I know not what to say.'

'You, at least, have no objection to our union?'

'None in the world, if she is agreeable; but as I told you before, I will use no coercion.'

'Thanks for your permission to woo your handsome daughter.'

'And I as sincerely thank you for the gentlemanly manner in which you have proposed for her hand. If you think proper you can see her immediately.'

Mabel was accordingly sent for, but could not be found.

Every imaginable corner about the house was searched, but in vain; at last Betty made the announcement that she had been seen going in the direction of Bridgehouse. This seemed satisfactory to her father, who briefly remarked she was in the habit of going there daily, but that it was usually later in the day before she went. With a smile on his lips and a curse in his heart Kennedy was constrained to leave. Mounting his horse he rode off at a furious pace in the direction which Betty had said Mabel had taken.

'If my fate depended upon Bruce's answer I would be confident of success,' he soliloquised as he rode along. 'But why not use his parental authority? It seems she has bewitched him as well as me. If I'm to be successful Cochrane must be removed, that's evident. The minx! only to think of her going every day to Bridgehouse; but at the first opportunity I'll remove the temptation out of her path. Ha! Mac, what the d—— are you doing here?' cried Kennedy, suddenly reining up his steed beside his henchman.

'Yesterday I was fishing, but to-day I'm setting snares. Come along and I'll tell you the news.'

CHAPTER III.

IF there are two ways of looking at everything, so there are different ways of reading many expressions. When Macnairston said he had been setting snares, Kennedy thought, naturally enough, it was for Davie Cochrane, whereas it was for the express purpose of trapping himself Macnairston had been plotting. Master and servant were both about an age, the same size and complexion, but their externals were the only resemblance between them. Mentally the servant left the master far in the shade.

During the period they were abroad they were pretty much on terms of equality, for Kennedy would enter into no undertaking without first consulting Mac, as he generally called him. When at Vienna their fortunes were at a very low ebb, and as Kennedy, as a sept of the powerful house of Culzean, had access to the best families, Macnairston suggested to him the propriety of replenishing their exchequer at the private gaming tables of the wealthy citizens. To facilitate this laudable project, Macnairston initiated his master, who was completely on the rocks, into all the mysterious tricks which can be done with cards; and as Macnairston was passed off as a distant relation of Kennedy's, they often played at the same table. They were invariably fortunate, for between them were established telegraphic signs, which enabled them to play into each other's hands, so that if Macnairston lost, Kennedy was sure to win. By following up this dishonourable practice they became rich; and when they considered they had stayed long enough in one city they removed to another. At last they reached Paris, and there a circumstance occurred which was destined, unfortunately, to work Kennedy's ruin. One of the houses these accomplished gentlemen resorted to often was that of Count de Larcy, who was reputed to keep the gayest establishment and the best wines in Paris, while his only daughter Julia was celebrated far and near for her accomplishments and rare beauty. Kennedy and Macnairston both made love to the Count's beauteous daughter, and Macnairston was the favourite suitor, which excited Kennedy's jealousy to a fearful degree. At last, fearful that his servant was going to carry off the coveted prize, he craved a private audience, and denounced Macnairston as a plebeian and a benedict, and the Count's doors were closed against him. Kennedy now had the field to himself, and the young lady being truly grateful to him for his friendly warning, he had little difficulty in ingratiating himself into her favour, and in a short time succeeded in accomplishing her ruin. In vain Macnairston craved to know the nature of his offence. His master told him he had been expelled the Count's house for making undue familiarity with the Lady Julia.

About this time Kennedy received a message from the Rector of St John's Kirk, Ayr, urging upon him the necessity of returning home instantly, as his father was dying.

Without informing the unfortunate Lady Julia, Kennedy began to prepare for his homeward journey; but Macnairston, being often in the company of Julia's valet, informed him of his master's intention of leaving soon for Scotland.

Upon being informed of this by her servant, the rage and despair of the ruined Julia was fearful to witness. The very fact of Kennedy's reticence was proof, strong as holy writ, that he meant to betray her. In her terrible distress she sent for Macnairston, and among other things told him of Kennedy's perfidy, thinking, no doubt, that he would espouse her quarrel.

Gladly would he have done so, but well he knew Kennedy would scorn to fight a duel with his servant. Instantly he would have left Kennedy's service, for the system which had replenished his master's coffers had enriched his own, but by doing so he relinquished any chance of revenging the perfidy he had been guilty of. He told Julia of the resolve he had taken; and her love, being so basely trampled on, was changed into the most implacable hatred, therefore she entered heart and soul into Macnairston's scheme, promising him a princely reward when it was accomplished. With this mutual understanding they parted.

Whatever dark thoughts were passing through Macnairston's mind, when he appeared before Kennedy his face wore as bland a smile as ever. That night they started for Scotland, and arrived at Greenan about two months before the opening of this tale.

'Did you see the young Laird of Bridgehouse to-day?' asked Kennedy, impatiently, at his servant whom he met as described at the end of the last chapter.

'I did, and he is elated about his approaching marriage.'

'His approaching marriage,' reiterated the Laird, 'surely he's dreaming, Mac?'

'Well, the day's not settled on yet, on which it's to take place, but it's well understood that it will be immediately.'

'The infernal, old, scheming, hypocritical wretch!' ejaculated Kennedy, fiercely, 'he never breathed a syllable of this to me.'

'To whom do you refer?'

'Bruce, of course. I am just coming from his house, and he gave me full permission to woo and win Mabel.'

'He did,' cried Macnairston, in well-feigned astonishment; 'well, it is hard to understand human nature. I tell thee, Laird, he both knows and approves of the marriage.'

'Did you see Mabel when at Bridgehouse?'

'I did not.'

'Ha! ha! just a *ruse* to get you out of the way. Go back now and you'll find they have been sporting with your feelings. I learned one thing when at Bridgehouse,' said Macnairston, in a sneering tone.

'Thou'rt a devil, Mac, and if you tempt me farther, I'll sheath my sword in your carcase.'

Macnairston cast a furtive, dark, malignant look at him and remained silent. His time for speaking had not yet come.

'What did you learn, knave, when at Bridgehouse?'

'That the beauteous Mabel and the brave Cochrane are to meet to-night.'

'Where?'

'Near Alloway Kirk.'

'Well, Mac, it will be their last meeting if you're willing to help me.'

'Me help you! well, you know, dear master, how ready I have always been to serve you.'

'And yourself at same time, Mac, but we'll not quarrel now.'

'I rather think not, especially when we have such important business to settle to-night.'

'You'll be sure and get the message conveyed to Mabel. Remember any bungling on your part will ruin the plot.'

'I'm aware of that, sir. Depend upon my tact and discretion. The road near Greenan is lonely and unfrequented.'

By this time they had arrived at the castle, and, as the understanding seemed to be perfect between them, they separated.

The afternoon wore wearily along, but at last the dial in the garden indicated the hour in which each had to assume their characters in the tragic drama about to be enacted.

'I'm going to bait the trap, Laird,' cried Macnairston, at the door of Kennedy's room; 'be sure and be at the rendezvous at the appointed hour.'

'Depend upon me, Mac, I'll be there.'

Macnairston walked down the court of the castle, humming a favourite Scottish ballad with the greatest indifference, while his master exclaimed, as he watched his retreating form, 'He's an invaluable servant.'

Regardless of the beauty of the scenery around him, Macnairston took the shortest way to Cunningpark, where Mr Bruce made him welcome, but scarcely in such a warm manner as usual. He informed him of Kennedy's visit and proposal, and characterised it as being strictly honourable.

'Had you and Mabel accepted his proposal, you would have found the villain out. However, it is nothing to me, Mr Bruce, how you settle the matter. I have only acted as a friend to you and fair Mabel, and if you do not follow my advice, it will neither make nor mar my fortune.'

'Don't be angry, Mac. I believe you have spoken disinterestedly in this affair,' said the confiding old man.

Macnairston next sought Mabel, and informed her that he had just left Bridgehouse, and that David had told him that it was impossible he could meet her at the Kirk to-night, as he had to go on important business to Dunure, but that, as he had something of importance to communicate, he would be glad to meet her on the road above Greenan about nine o'clock.

Mabel would never have dreamed of going so far, but she, like every other young lady, was all impatient to tell her lover of Kennedy's visit and proposal, so after reflecting a moment she said she would go.

Having arrived at Bridgehouse, Macnairston sought the young Laird, and prepared to play his last card.

'I have doleful news for you this evening,' began Macnairston, in a well-assumed voice and look of sorrow; " Kennedy was telling me before I left that he had a trap laid for Mabel to-night; and when I heard his diabolical scheme unfolded, I could not rest until I informed you of it."

'Gracious heaven! I don't understand you, man; tell me, in mercy, what you mean?'

'I can tell you but little further than this, that Mabel has been given to understand you cannot meet her at the Kirk, but that she is to see you on the path a little above Greenan. Of course Kennedy will be waiting for her in place of you, and bear the fair Mabel off to his eyrie.'

'Will he, the false-hearted craven! Then it will be over my corpse,' exclaimed the young Laird, as he rushed into the stable and brought forth a powerful horse.

'Give me another, and I'll accompany you, let the consequences be what they may.'

CHAPTER IV.

WHILE the incidents narrated in the last chapter were occurring at Bridgehouse, Mabel was hurrying along the road leading to Dunure. The last rays of the setting sun were lighting up the fleecy clouds afar to the westward, and giving to some the appearance of huge mountains, whose rifted summits were covered with snow, while others seemed great castles tinted with blue and gold. Immediately on her left, rose Brown Carrick Hill, covered with heather, hazel, broom, and whin, among which the mavis and blackbird poured forth their vespers, mingled with the lowing of kine and bleating of sheep. Occasionally a soft, cooling breeze came sighing over the placid sea, lifting gently, for a moment, the luxuriant tresses of her dark auburn hair, peeping beneath at her snowy neck, and then letting them fall gracefully over her shoulders—in those days chignons were unfashionable. What a pity!

Mabel was not gaudily dressed, but what we call tidy. Over her left arm she carried that indispensable article of a Scottish lassie's outfit—a tartan plaid. The very simplicity of her attire enhanced her loveliness, and proved the truth of the poet's words—

> 'Beauty needs not the foreign aid of ornaments,
> But is, when unadorned, adorned the most.'

As she skipped along over the velvet pathway she felt happy—as the young and innocent always do. It is only when sin has found an entrance into that most beautiful structure of Creative power—man—that we become wretched, faithless, hopeless. Mabel's hope was strong and brilliant as the roseate tints that lingered yet on the hills around her. Away in the future were glorious vistas through which she wandered with the idol of her heart—David Cochrane.

Along with the young Laird of Bridgehouse, how truthful seemed the words—

> 'With love, a cottage by a brook
> In some fair glen, is better far
> Than palaces, tho' grand they look,
> If won by fraud or deadly war.
> If love lights up the humblest cot,
> Then that's a holy, happy spot.'

As these thoughts swept pleasantly through her mind a sudden turn in the road brought her nearly face to face with a solitary horseman. Mabel walked to the side-path to allow the stranger to pass, but such evidently was not his intention, for reining up his steed, he sprang from the saddle, and before Mabel recovered her self-possession, he clasped his arms around her and struggled for a kiss. In a moment she recognized the hated Laird of Greenan, and renewed her struggles to free herself. Grasping her plaid he wound it quickly around her head, but not until she had awakened the sleeping echoes with a wild despairing cry for help. That cry for help was heard by Cochrane and Macnairston, and they lashed their steeds furiously forward to reach the place from which it proceeded. Long and bravely did Mabel struggle in the hands of her ruthless assaulter, but she was no match for such a powerful ruffian. At length she became insensible and sunk helplessly to the earth. Pantingly Kennedy lifted her up, threw her across the back of his well-trained horse, sprang into the saddle, and made off with the apparently lifeless maiden. Leaving the road, he struck across the fields for Greenan, but not without being seen by his pursuers. Leaving the road, at a point further down, they scoured across the country, and at last got between Kennedy and the castle. So busily was he engaged holding Mabel and managing his horse that he never observed the horsemen approaching until Cochrane shouted, 'Cowardly dastard! I have caught you at last.' As he cried this he rode furiously up, brandishing his sword.

Seeing there was no chance of escape, Kennedy threw Mabel from the horse, and, drawing his sword, prepared to defend himself. The next moment they were engaged in deadly conflict, but the inexperienced Laird of Bridgehouse was no match for the well-trained Laird of Greenan.

Macnairston watched with knitted brows the contest, without uttering a word, until he saw Cochrane fall from his horse; then, rushing forward, he exclaimed—'Now, Kennedy, you and I must square accounts.'

'Base-born hound, I'll soon send thee to thy long account!' cried Kennedy, panting with passion; but, embittered as he was against his treacherous henchmen, his strength was nearly gone.

'That's for Lady Julia, Laird,' cried Macnairston, as he passed his sword through his right arm, ' and that's for myself,' he exultingly exclaimed, as he severed the left one from his body. Kennedy, with a savage curse on his lips, fell beside the Laird of Bridgehouse.

Without casting a glance at his three victims, he turned his horse's head, exclaiming, as he rode off the field, 'They may lie there till they rot for me.'

Mabel had recovered from her state of unconsciousness, and, seeing Macnairston ride off, she gathered courage to rise and look about her. She saw Cochrane lying in a pool of blood, and Kennedy stretched beside him. Raising her lover's head, she saw with infinite joy that life was not extinct, although he was dangerously wounded in the left side. Staunching the flow of blood as well as she could, she laid his head on her bosom and sobbed piteously. Although it was nearly dark, the cries of the combatants and the clashing of swords had attracted to the spot two of the serfs belonging to Greenan.

'Holy Virgin! girl, who has done this?' exclaimed the strongest and fiercest looking of the two.

'It was Macnairston,' sobbed Mabel. 'For God's sake, help them to the castle.'

'This is strange, maiden. Where is Mac?' As the stout retainer said this he sprang on the back of Kennedy's horse, and then cried at his companion to give him a grip of his master's hand; unitedly they lifted him up. 'Set the damsel now on the other horse, and try and lift that youth from the earth.' This was a work of some difficulty, but at last it was accomplished, and they at once started for the castle.

A messenger was instantly despatched to Ayr for Father Forbes, one of the priests belonging to St John's.

At this period clergymen were not only cures of the soul, but of the body; therefore, when Father Forbes arrived at Greenan, late at night, he set instantly about examining the state of Cochrane and Kennedy. The former, with proper care, he said, would recover; but Kennedy's was a hopeless case, although, he said, he might live to morning. Doing his best to restore Kennedy to consciousness, by applying restoratives, he at last opened his eyes, gazed wildly about him, and asked for wine.

'Give him whatever he asks for,' said the holy man; 'he has but a few hours to live, and I wish to hear his confession before he dies.'

'Can money not save my life?' groaned the dying man.

'Not all the wealth of the world; prepare to meet thy God,' said the priest, in a solemn voice.

'Does Cochrane live?'

'He does. What of that?'

'Give me more wine. Is he here? Ask him if he forgives me?' gasped Kennedy.

'He forgives thee as he hopes to be forgiven.

'That's well! Macnairston, curse him.'

'Hush,' said the priest, interrupting him; 'you must forgive your enemies.'

'I cannot. I'm immensely rich: you'll find my gold in a strong oaken chest in my bedroom. Give Mabel Bruce for dower a thousand pieces of gold; the remainder of my wealth I leave to found a church to be called St Leonard. Dost thou hear, priest?'

'Yes, yes, my son; say on.'

'It is to be built in the vicinity of Ayr; and the officiating chaplain is to offer up a mass weekly for the repose of my soul.'

'It shall be faithfully performed.'

Kennedy fell back on the pillow and breathed with difficulty.

'Thy end is approaching, friend; would'st thou care to speak to me privately?'

The only audible reply to this was the name of Macnairston, but whether he cursed or blessed him was long disputed by the priests of St Leonards.

The proud, imperious Kennedy gave a groan, quivered convulsively, and expired.

'*Requiescat in pace,*' muttered the priest, as he made the sign of the cross, and ordered one of the servants to light the way to Kennedy's bed room, to seal his wealth in the name of the church.

The young Laird of Bridgehouse was removed from Greenan Castle on the morning following the death of Kennedy. With gentle nursing he recovered from the effects of his wound in the course of a few weeks, and shortly afterwards he was united to the Rose of the Isle. They lived to wander with their children's children along the sunny slopes of Brown Carrick Hill, and along the banks of Doon, which has since been rendered classic by the immortal Burns.

Macnairston found his way to Paris, and at once sought the abode of the fair Lady de Larcy. Her father, hearing of her disgrace, died sorrowing. Being thus left to the freedom of her own will, she ran headlong into every excess of the gay capital. For a while she seemed pleased with the attentions of Macnairston, but, wearying of his jealous superintendence, she quietly disposed of him. He went one night to bed rather tipsy, and in the morning was found dead.

We must now draw the curtain and retire; but to the lover of the picturesque, we would say that around the auld toun of Ayr, there are many sweet haunts, with hallowed recollections, but none are in our opinion more worthy of a visit than the storm-beaten, crumbling ruins of Greenan Castle.

DUNN AND WRIGHT, PRINTERS, GLASGOW.